# THE BIG CHEESE

## OLD SCHOOL MYSTERIES
### BOOK 2

ANDREA C. NEIL

*For Julie and Kim…*
*…and another 40 years of friendship*

# CHAPTER 1

Delphine Lougheed watched the dancers swirl around the ballroom to Glenn Miller's "Moonlight Serenade." As she took a break from the dancing for a song or two, she swayed where she stood, transported to another time. A time when her youth and vigor seemed endless, as did adventure and excitement. Life had seemed simpler so long ago.

But even in her younger years, Delphine's life hadn't been all that simple. As a spy for an elite, top-secret agency called the Falls, her days had been filled with danger and her nights with … more danger. Sometimes when she looked back, she couldn't believe she'd survived it all. Yet here she was, retired and trying to live her best life. Which included dancing.

Her dance club, the Trotting Foxes, met several times a week at the Sassy Steppers Studio in Pasadena. They practiced for upcoming competitions, and also invited non-members to join in the fun on open studio nights, like tonight. Ballroom dancing was Delphine's favorite hobby, and she loved watching everyone move around the room. But it was even more fun to be out on the floor. The excitement of the moment, the interplay between the partners and their surroundings, the music … It all came together to create an experience that she loved and craved.

These days, she couldn't think of a single thing she'd rather be doing than dancing; it provided her with a much-needed outlet, ever since she had, in theory, retired from the Falls a few years earlier. Not that anyone ever fully retired from her line of work—assuming they made it to her age without getting killed first. She wasn't technically on the payroll anymore, but she still got asked to participate in an advisory capacity from time to time.

In her younger years, her craving for excitement had been indulged by the work she did as a super-spy. International intrigue, everyday espionage, travel, and danger had all been part of the job description. From royalty to rednecks and swamps to staterooms, she'd seen it all.

She still missed her job, truth be told. It had been dangerous work, but rewarding. One wrong move and disaster might strike. Torture, imprisonment … even death. Now, in retirement, she relied on ballroom dancing to fill the void left by quitting the job she'd loved so much. These days, the only danger she faced was a broken hip or ankle. But she'd never made a misstep back then and she wasn't about to make one now.

Delphine spotted her usual dance partner, Walter Shipley, across the room from where she stood with her friend Marvis as they put out a few snacks that the club provided as treats for guests. Walter had also worked at the Falls, but unlike Delphine, who'd retired, Shipley was still employed by the organization. He was a blatant womanizer, but on the dance floor, all that mattered was the fact he was one of the most elegant dancers she'd ever known.

Shipley stood chatting with another club regular, Mitzi Bouffant, and Delphine watched as his professionally whitened teeth glowed when he smiled at her. Mitzi ran a hand down Ship's arm and laughed as if her life depended on it, and her trademark sparkly, dangly earrings swung wildly with each guffaw.

"She better not be trying to steal him away," Delphine muttered.

Marvis laughed. "If I didn't know you so well, I'd say you're sweet on him."

Delphine scoffed. "How many times do I have to tell you, I'm only interested in Shipley out there on the floor. If he weren't the best dancer in the club, I wouldn't give a rat's patootie about him."

"*You* are the best dancer in the club," said Marvis.

Delphine thought about being modest for a moment, but it was true, and everyone knew it. "I just want to win our next regional competition," she said. "That's the only reason I care."

"Sure," said Marvis, and handed her a paper cup filled with something red and syrupy.

Delphine took one sip of the questionable liquid and winced. "When are we going to stop serving this abhorrence?"

"As soon as people start contributing more to our snack budget. Value-sized containers of powdered Fruit Smacko is all the club has money for," said Marvis. "You know how hard it is to get anyone to shell out cash." She took an FDA-warning-sized gulp from her own cup and shivered.

Delphine did know. Despite being based in a city as nice as Pasadena, the Trotting Foxes were notorious penny pinchers. She made a mental note to spring for something healthier the next time she was out shopping. The last thing the dance club needed, or the studio, which was owned by Marvis and her husband Franko, was to be sued for giving someone liver damage.

Something shiny and bouncy caught Delphine's attention. "Who is that?" she asked, nodding at a woman who stood near the DJ's table talking to Franko. The woman wore a floor-length, midnight-blue gown, much like her own. But the similarities between Delphine's dress and the mystery guest's gown ended at color and length. The buxom, dark-haired woman's sleek dress was partially covered in sequins, unlike Delphine's. And it showed a lot more cleavage.

"No idea," said Marvis. "But she started coming a few weeks ago, while you were on vacation on the East Coast."

"Hmm." Delphine watched the woman, who tossed her head back and displayed a big, easy smile, her hair bouncing almost in slow motion, like the glamorous women in those shampoo commercials. It was the kind of move reserved for when a person knew the whole room had its eye on them. Which it did. "Hmm," she said again, and continued to watch as Shipley tore himself away from Mitzi and fell into the other woman's gravitational pull.

Delphine held the cup of Fruit Smacko at arm's length and walked to a nearby folding table, where she exchanged the sugary death liquid for her stainless-steel water bottle. Water, hydration beverage of (dance) champions.

There was no mistaking the bottle for anyone else's—her eight-year-old granddaughter Zooey had covered it with stickers from the Sierra Club, World Wildlife Federation, and multiple National Parks. Delphine couldn't even remember what color the bottle was underneath them all.

A moment before, the only thing she had been wondering about was whether or not she should dance with Ship one more time. But as she looked around the room, she discovered there were more important things to ponder, like why her former boss was standing by the front door of the dance studio.

Richard Dere, manager of the Southern California branch of the Falls. She hadn't seen him in months, and here he was, blessing the studio with his presence. Back in the day, he'd been an up-and-coming young agent who rocketed to the top of the agency faster than you could say *equal opportunity*. Now in his mid-sixties, thinning hair stood in wisps atop the egg-shaped head attached to his pear-shaped body. His suit was new, and his money was old.

Richard had won multiple awards and was the overseer of one of the agency's most prominent regions. He was clever, but also manipulative, and Delphine was certain he'd been promoted so many times due to chicanery rather than merit. And he'd criticized Delphine at every step of her career.

It came as no surprise when he walked over to the woman in the blue dress and planted a big wet kiss on her face. Of course— his latest wife. Delphine began to get that feeling in the pit of her stomach. The one she relied on so heavily whenever she found herself in dangerous situations. The one that had saved her life many times.

She took a drink from her water bottle and closed her eyes to think. Should she try to sneak out to avoid possible engagement with Richard? Should she simply ignore him if he happened to notice her? Or maybe it would be best to grab Ship and start dancing…

"Hello, Delphine."

Too late to choose.

She opened her eyes and there stood Richard, who reached out to shake her hand but never quite looked at her face. It wasn't like when her granddaughter Griffin didn't make eye contact—the girl was a touch socially awkward, or whatever they called it nowadays. Richard, on the other hand, avoided Delphine's gaze for another reason. He never did like the way she could see right through him and all his administrative banana oil. And she knew this because she could see right through him.

"Always a pleasure, Richard," she said as she smiled and accepted his limp handshake. Just because she didn't trust the man as far as she could throw him (which was still a fair distance, on a good day), didn't mean he had to know that. "What brings you here tonight?"

He looked in the direction of the woman in the blue dress, who still had a Shipley stuck to her. "Juliette loves ballroom dancing. I told her this was the best group in California, so naturally she wanted to join," he said without looking at Delphine.

"But she's not dancing," said Delphine.

"She says her ankle hurts tonight."

They watched Ship lead Juliette through the crowd. She wobbled a few times on her very high heels, and when they were in the center of the room, Ship took her in his arms and pulled her close. *Ankle schmankle*, thought Delphine.

After twenty seconds of what could loosely be termed dancing, it became clear to Delphine that the woman knew nothing about it.

"She's a natural," said Delphine as she watched the woman step on Ship's feet several times.

Richard beamed. "She sure is!"

"Is she number five or number six?"

His smile drooped a little. "Six. No, five. No—yes, five. It'll be two years next month."

"I'm sure this one will stick. Anyway, I'm surprised to find you out and about," she added.

"Yes, well, they don't want me staying so late at the office anymore, so I guess I have extra free time."

"Great," said Delphine, imagining the possibility of him showing up more often at the Sassy Steppers. It was not a pleasant image.

"The higher-ups want to see me retire," he said. "After I've taken them the best years … Since my career … I mean, after I've given them the best years of my life."

"Retirement's not so bad," said Delphine. She'd been able to spend time with her youngest granddaughter, Zooey, and do a little traveling for pleasure. Although her last "vacation" had been a trip to Florida to bail Griffin's other grandma out of jail, and that hadn't gone very smoothly. "Most of the time."

"I'm going to try to stay on another year or two," said Richard. His eyes never left Juliette as she stomped her way across the dance floor, using Ship's feet as landing pads.

Delphine noticed a look of concern cross Richard's face. He had once been a handsome man, but he looked like he'd been doing a lot more worrying lately.

"What are you really doing here, Richard?" she asked.

"I told you, Juliette wanted to dance."

"Yes, that's why she is here. But that's not why you are here."

He laughed. "Oh Delphine, always so suspicious. You always were one to jump to conclusions. One of your biggest flaws as a female agent."

Years of dealing with Richard and men like him made it possible for her to let the *female* part of his observation roll off her back. Regardless of her gender, he might have been right though. Maybe she had been too impetuous a few times. But her suspicions and instincts had saved her far more times than they had hindered her.

In any case, she wasn't going to fall for his misdirection; she'd stopped doing that years ago. Something had brought Richard to the studio on this night, and she wanted to know what it was.

"We'll see," she said in a neutral tone.

They watched the dancers move around the floor until the song ended. Ship looked at his feet and winced until Juliette began bouncing and clapping, at which point he stood transfixed with his gaze locked somewhere other than his own feet.

Richard didn't seem to notice, or care. He said, "Since Juliette loves to dance, I thought it would be something we could do together. You know, find more common interests as a couple."

Delphine assumed that two of Richard and Juliette's common interests were money and carnal desire. Perhaps dancing could be a third.

"I do remember you being a decent dancer," she said, letting another lie escape her mouth.

"Yes, well," he said, puffing out his chest a bit. "To be honest, I'm also thinking of buying this studio."

"Is that so," said Delphine, intrigued. She wondered if the Sassy Steppers Dance Studio was for sale or if he planned to make an unsolicited bid. Interesting comment, either way.

"Yep, I want to do some more investing. I used to own one of those toasted sub shops, but my doctor told me if I ate one more slice of processed lunch meat, my intestines would explode. So I thought, why not a dance studio? It could be a good business hobby. A smart ... A good investment as well as a hobby, I mean. I'm having my money guy do an improbability study."

Delphine's left eyebrow rose. "Do you mean a feasibility study?"

"No."

Delphine shook off his comment and chalked it up to his unusual speech patterns. Everyone who worked with him had trouble with his communication style until they got used to it, and Delphine had learned to roll with it as best she could. Sometimes it took a minute to figure out what he meant though.

Richard wanted to own a dance studio? Back in the day, all agents had been required to know a few basic steps, so they could fit in at formal functions. That was how she'd first learned, and her mandatory lessons turned into a hobby. But she'd never known Richard to be a fan of dancing of any kind. And now he wanted to buy not just any dance studio, but the one she went to regularly.

"Why this one?" she asked.

"It's close to home," he said, and Delphine remembered that he lived in the area, like she did.

"Ah. Well, a lot of people who come here are very particular," she explained, thinking mostly of herself. "If you decide to buy, I would caution you against making any sweeping changes."

Richard looked at her and smiled his pointy-toothed smile. "Maybe sweeping changes is what this place needs."

"Maybe," she said, doubtful but wanting to appear neutral.

"Well," said Richard, lifting onto the balls of his feet for a second. "I think I'll go try some of that punch everyone's been raving about."

# CHAPTER 2

The rest of the evening went well. Delphine danced one more number with Walter Shipley, and at the end of the song she considered "accidentally" stepping on his foot with the heel of her shoe, just for fun. But he would probably be plenty sore already without her help, thanks to Juliette Dere's fancy footwork.

She also danced once with Franko Schlott, Marvis's husband, and once with Richard, at his insistence.

The last time she and Richard had danced together was during an undercover operation at a black-tie gala in Santiago, fifteen years back. The event was to honor up-and-coming Chilean actors —at least that was the official purpose. The Falls had placed agents on site to spy on one of the actors, who was suspected of price fixing in the wool-sweater import market.

The event had been a singular night for Delphine. She got to meet the ultra-famous actor Pedro Bernal. Pedro had been charming and beguiling, and Delphine came back to California with a few memories that were impossible to top, the details of which would never pass her lips.

When everyone else had left and the final dregs from the punch bowl had been used to clean the drain of the kitchenette sink, Delphine, Ship, Richard, and Juliette closed up the studio with Marvis and Franko.

The parking lot was still full of cars since the strip mall also contained a twenty-four-hour laundromat/bar, a small improv club called No And, and a regional office of ScriptDoctor, an international chain that helped everyone from waiters to investment bankers write their film screenplays. Even though this was Pasadena and not downtown LA, the shop was often mistaken for a pill farm, so there were always interesting people milling around outside. It was sometimes hard to tell the pillheads from the scriptwriters—they were all a little jittery.

The six dancers stood on the sidewalk outside the studio for a moment, saying their goodbyes. Ship left first, heading in the same direction as Delphine had parked. She must have gotten a spot near his Buick SUV, she realized.

"Darling, let's walk Delphine to her car," Richard said to Juliette.

Juliette gave Delphine a thorough head-to-toe inspection. "I'll wait in the Jag," she said in a French accent, and teetered off in the opposite direction Ship had gone.

Something in Juliette's eyes gave Delphine pause. Juliette's gaze seemed to flit over her with more than disdain—there was something else there. Delphine felt guilty for a split-second, as if Juliette knew the older woman was judging her for being Richard's fifth—no, sixth—wife. Or had it been a look of pity? Or recognition? Something about the younger woman seemed almost familiar.

"I'll be right there," he told his wife. "I just want to make sure she's safe."

"I don't need you to accompany me," Delphine said. She tried to remain civil, while inside she seethed at his remark. He must have forgotten that she could kill a man as easily as she could reapply lipstick and did not need an escort through a Pasadena parking lot. Chivalry could kiss her senior-citizen butt.

"Oh no, it's my pleasure," he said. "We wouldn't want anything to happen to you."

She wasn't so sure that was true, but gave in to his attempt at politeness.

"I'm parked over there." She pointed in the direction Ship had gone.

They were silent for a few steps, and Delphine could hear Richard's trademark uneven gait as his custom-made leather shoes scraped lightly on the asphalt. *Scrape. Thump.* One of his legs was shorter than the other, although a few Falls staffers had spread a rumor a few years back that he had a wooden leg. But Delphine had seen him in shorts when they'd been on assignment in Monaco once, and knew it wasn't true.

"Do you still see Kenji?" he asked as they walked.

"From time to time." She actually saw Kenji all the time, but that was one more thing Richard didn't need to know. She thought about changing the subject by introducing a more neutral topic, like the state of that year's mango crop in Mexico, but before she had a chance, she noticed Ship standing next to his car a few rows over, looking at something with great concentration. She followed his gaze to see two figures dressed in black, standing by a parked car. Her car.

Delphine picked up her pace and made a beeline for her dark-blue Mercedes E Class, forgetting Richard was with her.

"What is it?" he asked from a few steps back.

"Not sure." She felt for the outline of her handgun in her purse —her Colt King Cobra snub nose .38 was still there. It may have been overkill to bring it to a dance studio, but it was a reassuring accessory. Richard caught up with her and so did Ship, who by then had noticed them speed by.

Delphine got close enough to confirm that the two men were in fact standing next to her Mercedes, but seconds later, they spotted her and ran down the row of parked vehicles to the street, where they jumped into an idling black Mustang. It sped off down the boulevard with a throaty roar.

"What was that about?" asked Ship when they'd all arrived at her car.

Richard was out of breath. Delphine and Ship were not.

"No idea," said Delphine. She checked the passenger side of her Mercedes—there was no sign of damage or forced entry.

"They … were probably trying to steal it," said Richard, still panting.

Ship nodded. "It is a sweet ride."

"If either of you makes another crack about how I got paid too much for doing the same job as Ship here, you will regret it for a very long time to come." She pulled her car keys from the outside pocket of her purse with a scowl.

Over the years she'd heard it all. She was fairly certain she had made less than Ship for doing the same job, even though she still made a good living. But a woman who got paid a decent wage and happened to be savvy with money often suffered the fate of being considered unscrupulous or just freakishly lucky. Usually the passive-aggressive berating was done under the guise of jokes. They were never very funny.

She looked at the driver's side door, but there was no sign of forced entry or smudged fingerprints anywhere on that side either. "I don't think they were trying to steal it," she said.

"Of course they were," said Richard, waving a hand at her. "What else would they want?"

That part flummoxed Delphine also.

Ship lifted his chin and wrinkled his nose. "What's that smell?"

Delphine sniffed and sure enough, a pungent, almost musty smell wafted through their immediate vicinity. "Maybe someone's got some dirty clothes in their car that they're too drunk to take into the laundromat," she said.

But that didn't seem to be good enough for Ship. He began to walk around the car. "It's stronger back here."

"I'm sure it's nothing. It's fine, you both can go. Richard, Juliette is waiting for you." Delphine wished Richard and Ship would leave her be so she could get home. Whatever the mystery men had been trying to accomplish had been thwarted, she was sure of it. Now all she wanted was to go home, have a snack, and take a bath.

But Ship circled the car again, this time stopping at the left rear tire. Richard and Delphine followed, and the smell was indeed stronger at the back of the car. Ship pointed to her trunk and looked at her. Delphine pulled her keys from her purse and popped the deck lid. And there in the back of her nice, clean Mercedes were four, 100-pound wheels of honest-to-goodness French Beaufort d'Alpage cheese, one of the most expensive dairy delicacies in the world.

That could only mean one thing.

The Big Cheese was back in town.

# CHAPTER 3

Delphine took a drink from her coffee cup and glared at Richard Dere, who watched her from the other side of an elegant boardroom table. They sat in the conference room of the Falls regional office, not too far from Pasadena. Two manila folders lay before him—one thin and new, the other fatter and a little worn around the edges. A lot like Richard, she mused.

The thin folder must have been the beginnings of a case file; the second, larger one was probably her personnel file. Or part of it, anyway. Her complete work history with the organization would fill several bankers boxes by now.

Richard stared at her left ear, tapping an index finger on the thinner folder. He had been late to the meeting, making Delphine wait for him in the conference room alone with Walter Shipley. Fifteen minutes after they were supposed to start and fourteen minutes after her patience had worn thin, he'd arrived with his assistant, Judy.

The previous night had been a long one since Richard had insisted on calling in a team to go over every inch of Delphine's car as well as all the wheels of Beaufort d'Alpage. The cheese had been impounded, of course. Without any papers to confirm its origin, or proof that import tariffs had been paid, the four giant wheels of top-shelf dairy product were essentially illegal.

After three hours of waiting in the Sassy Steppers parking lot, Richard finally let her go home with the understanding that she would have to come in for questioning the next morning. And here they were.

Richard took a deep breath and looked at the table as he spoke. "As you know, the Falls takes matters of national finance to utmost secure. I mean, we make people money. I…"

Judy gave her boss the side eye as he struggled for words, and Delphine's patience wore even thinner. Everyone had gotten used to Richard floundering for words and considered it a tolerable eccentricity, but it was still annoying as all get-out.

"Our purpose," he began again, "is to uphold the safety and sovereignty of the assets we are assigned to protect. You were not able to produce papers that can attest to your legal right to be in possession of any imported cheese products. As such, the four wheels of Beaufort d'Alpage that were discovered in your car last night have been confiscated until their origin can be confirmed."

"Where is the cheese now?" Delphine asked him.

Richard's expression remained impassive, save for a hint of a twitch of his left eyelid. Delphine tried not to smile.

"I am not at liberty to say, that's official business," he said. "And you are here for me to ask questions to for. I mean, I am here for you … You will answer my questions, not the other way around."

Over breakfast that morning, she had considered bringing her attorney, Frances Flance, with her. But she felt confident that she would be able to handle this meeting on her own and there was no need to disturb one of her best friends so early in the morning. It was already 9:45, but Frances was a night owl, plus she might have been out of the country on a cruise anyway. The woman claimed she was semi-retired, and spent over half her time on cruise ships, but she often worked from her state room and flew home in time to make her court dates.

"Why is Walter here?" Delphine asked, pointing at Shipley, who was scratching something off the surface of the table with his fingernail. He looked up at the mention of his name.

"I just reminded you that I am the only one who will be asking the questions here," said Richard. "Now please tell us where you got the cheese that we found in the trunk of your car last night."

"What cheese?" asked Delphine.

Judy put her hand to her mouth to cover a smile as Richard made a sour face at Delphine.

"I'll say it again. That is not my cheese, nor do I have any knowledge of how the cheese got in my car. I can't even lift one of those wheels." Her statements were only partly true. She didn't know how the cheese had gotten in her car, but she could lift a wheel by herself. Still, it came in handy to play the old-lady card sometimes.

"Then who moved your cheese?" asked Walter Shipley, who sat three seats to Richard's right. No one said anything.

Delphine scrutinized Ship. Clad today in leisure slacks and a golf shirt, he cut a trim figure. If only he'd stop dying his hair. And she wasn't sure, but it looked as if he went for spray tans on the regular. He wasn't one of the smartest guys around, but he was loyal—an important quality for a Falls agent. Plus, he was quick on his feet.

But if he wasn't such a phenomenal dancer, she wouldn't give him the time of day. The man attracted women at a rate slightly below the speed of sound, and for the life of her she couldn't figure out why. Even before age and gravity had done a number on him, he'd never been all that handsome.

"Again, why is he here?" she asked, glaring at him.

"I still work here," said Ship. "Richard thought—"

"No one needs to know what I think. I mean, that's not her business, Ship." Richard turned to Delphine. "He is a key witness."

"He's not an active agent. He shouldn't be here," she insisted. It was common knowledge that Ship had been put on administrative leave. It was the only way the agency had been able to get him out of the office without firing him, since he refused to retire, and on paper he was still in good standing as an agent.

"I saw what I saw," said Ship. "Or should I say, I smelled what I smelled." He laughed and looked around for encouragement. No one said anything.

Richard thumbed through a sheaf of papers he had pulled from the thin manila folder. "Let's go over this again."

"For the millionth time, Richard, I've told you everything. Besides, whatever I say doesn't matter. We both know you've got your mind made up," she said.

"That's ridiculous." Richard closed the thin folder with a flourish and slid it and her personnel file to his right along the sleek tabletop, where they came to a stop in front of Judy, who sat in the next chair. "Let's just go by the facts."

"Okay, let's," said Delphine. "We spotted two men standing by my car, and they took off when they saw us. Somehow Shipley determines my car smells—"

"It did smell!" barked Ship.

"So we open the trunk," continued Delphine without looking away from Richard. "And we find four wheels of rare, expensive French cheese."

"That's not suspicious to you?" asked Ship.

One day, Delphine would thank Walter Shipley for the generous contribution to mankind of perfecting his firm grasp of the obvious. But not today.

"Of course it's suspicious," said Delphine. "But not in the way Richard is suggesting."

"I'm not suggesting anything," said Richard.

"Really?" said Delphine. Men were so predictable. They would argue with you just for the sake of arguing.

"Okay, yes. I'm suggesting you. I mean, something. I'm being suggestive. Anyway, in light of everything that's happened, it's definitely suspicious," said Richard.

Delphine wanted to reach across the table and smash Richard's nose into the polished wood. Then she made a mental note to let her therapist know she still had some anger issues to work through. (Everyone in LA had a therapist, even—or especially—semi-retired field agents. Almost everyone in LA had anger issues too.)

"That was over thirty years ago," she said without so much as a quiver in her voice.

"Maybe you were right back then," Richard said, narrowing his eyes at her. "Maybe we never did catch the Big Cheese after all."

Ship gasped. "Do you think she's back?"

Richard was referring to the cheese smuggling ring they'd been assigned to take down in the early eighties—operation Big Cheese. Someone had been bringing large amounts of expensive, high-quality French cheeses into the States without paying any tariffs on them, and the team's objective was to find the responsible party and bring them to justice as quietly as possible. They never found out what country, government, or shadow agency had instigated the project. Orders were orders, and agents always did as instructed.

The team had consisted of Delphine, her partner Kenji Yamamoto, Ship, and the Falls' foremost rare-cheese expert, Simon Pegbottam. Several private citizens worked with them as informants or support personnel, including a woman named Sylvie Lowenstein. Delphine had been the team leader, reporting to Richard. It was only the second time she'd been chosen to lead an operation, but it would be far from the last.

Progress had been slow, almost nonexistent, despite Delphine's herculean efforts to uncover any trace of whoever was in charge of the mysterious group. The enigmatic individual who spearheaded the whole thing was referred to as the Big Cheese, or sometimes as le Grande Fromage, since the cheeses in question were of French origin.

And then it happened.

On one cold and rainy November Thursday, while Delphine, Simon, and Ship were undercover at an exclusive cheese shop in Beverly Hills, Simon had left the store without his partners noticing. When Ship went looking for him, he found the agent in the alley behind the store, shot dead.

The following Monday, four months after being assigned to the case, Richard announced that Sylvie had been Big Cheese all along. He told them she'd also killed Simon. Then she'd disappeared without a trace. They were instructed by their higher-ups to terminate the case, and the project was shelved. Delphine, Kenji, and Ship started a new operation that took them to Peru for six months on a non-culinary mission. No one ever saw or heard from Sylvie Lowenstein again.

But Delphine could never let the case go. Simon's death had devastated her, as had the project's abrupt abandonment.

She believed the real ringleader was still out there somewhere, unaccounted for. It had never felt right to pin it on Sylvie Lowenstein; she could not have been the Big Cheese. Delphine was less sure about whether the woman was responsible for Simon's death, but it still seemed like a long shot. Blaming everything on Sylvie had been too easy, too convenient. No one ever found any proof that Sylvie was in charge. No one had found any proof of anything, and every time Delphine tried to bring it up with Richard, he always repeated the same story. Sylvie was the Big Cheese and that was that.

The project was shut down, the files locked away, and the subject melted into obscurity like a slice of warm Havarti on a tuna melt. It was still a tender spot for Delphine, however.

But after all this time … Could the Big Cheese really be back?

Richard looked at Delphine from across the table, but only for a second before diverting his eyes to his hands, now steepled on the table. "Anything is possible. Maybe we were mistaken about Sylvie. Maybe the real Big Cheese is closer than we think." He eyed her again.

Delphine did not like his tone or what his statement implied, and leaned forward to say something but changed her mind at the last second. The less she said now, the better. She didn't need Frances there to tell her that.

Shipley's eyes went wide, but he stayed silent too, and the gap in conversation grew longer. Judy began to fidget. Richard picked up the thin folder again. He opened it, riffled through the contents, then tossed it back at his assistant. This time it slid until it landed in front of Shipley, who reached for it but was too slow for Judy's quick reflexes.

Delphine smoothed the front of her blazer. "Are you going to charge me with anything?"

"Not yet," said Richard. "We still haven't determined the origin of the Beaufort d'Alpage. Until then, we'll be watching you."

She looked Richard in the eye and waited until he finally met her gaze. "Likewise."

Delphine and Judy stayed seated until the two men had left the room. Delphine could tell the woman had been pretending to organize a few sheets of paper as Richard and Ship shuffled out. It was doubtful the two men had noticed Judy's tactic though, or that she looked nervous. Why bother paying attention to what was right under their noses? But Delphine saw it. She waited patiently for Judy to reveal her reason for staying.

Judy rearranged the papers again and put them back into the thin folder. She opened her mouth to say something, but Richard's head appeared in the open doorway before she could speak.

"Judy, let's go. I need your help with the moffeecaker," he said, and his head disappeared.

Judy sighed and stood up, hugging the folders to her chest. "I have to go."

"Aren't you close to retirement?" asked Delphine.

"Not close enough," said Judy.

# CHAPTER 4

Delphine parked her car in her garage and decided to check the mailbox before going inside. She stopped to admire the century plants growing along her driveway. Drought-resistant beauties, they were. No weeding required in the new, parched California.

She desperately wanted a bath since she hadn't gotten one the night before. Baths always made her feel better. But then she thought of her granddaughter Zooey and the girl's passion for environmental causes. Zooey kept telling her baths were wasteful. Delphine knew it was true, and each year she saw more evidence of the havoc that humans wreaked on the planet. Sometimes it was so hard not to think of the Earth as a giant dumpster fire. Especially in her line of work.

How could things have gone so wrong in the course of twenty-four hours? One moment she was enjoying an evening of dancing and practicing for the next club dance competition. The next moment, she was having to defend herself in a smuggling case.

Where *was* Sylvie these days? Maybe the Big Cheese was back. Or maybe he had never stopped his operation. And why would he come after Delphine, after all this time? She had so many questions, she couldn't keep them straight. Her head was swimming in cheese.

In her mind, the Big Cheese had to be a man. But why? Was she being sexist by making that assumption? Taking a thirty-thousand-foot view of the situation, maybe she simply hoped a woman would have more sense, or better things to do, than be involved with something as ridiculous as a cheese smuggling operation. Yes, it was most assuredly a man.

No mail delivery yet, but she could feel that someone was watching her, so she walked across the street to Kenji's house. He was raking invisible leaves in his own pea-gravel-and-succulent front yard. She knew he knew what had happened.

"How'd you hear?" she asked.

Kenji stopped his meditative gardening and leaned one elbow on the top of the rake's wooden handle. "Please."

She admired his grey eyes. They were a few shades darker than his silver hair, which was now long enough over his ears to make him dangerously handsome. He had always been handsome though. They'd been partners in the field for over twenty-five years, and at some point—long after her beloved husband Charles passed away—their partnership changed from professional to something more. Those kinds of relationships were forbidden by management, but they were spies and good at hiding things. They'd made it work for many years until Delphine retired, and the romantic aspect of their relationship began to ebb.

Kenji had stayed on with the Falls a few more years, and they lost touch for a while. When an unfortunate mishap led to his replacement partner's untimely death, Kenji retired too. And then one day, a couple years ago, Delphine came home from a vacation to Santorini and found Kenji living in the house across the street. They fell into an easy routine, and within days it was as if they'd been neighbors forever. Their friendship rekindled, but the romance never had.

Delphine looked at him but said nothing, waiting for him to talk. You couldn't rush Kenji. If you tried, he'd make you regret it —by leading you in logic circles, barraging you with his own questions, or using any number of other exasperating tactics.

He took a deep breath before speaking. "I don't have much to tell you. I heard what happened, but nothing more."

"The Big Cheese is back," she said.

"Yes. It would appear so."

They were silent for a few beats before Delphine said what they were both thinking. "It's possible he never left."

Kenji stared at the gravel at his feet.

"But why now? Why implicate me?" A car went by, and Delphine jumped. It was a bad sign if she was this nervous. It felt like she was reliving the old days in more ways than one.

"As for the first question, you know as well as I do that there are only a handful of motives for why men become desperate enough to take action."

Delphine nodded, understanding his statement.

"As for the second question," Kenji continued, "heck if I know."

Suddenly she was hit by a rush of memories and emotions and physical sensations. It was as if just like that, she was back in her prime, experiencing the thrill and excitement of a high-stakes game.

"You are enjoying this, aren't you," said Kenji, cocking his head at her.

"I hadn't realized how easy it could be to get drawn back in. Don't you ever feel the pull?"

"That depends. Are you referring to feeling the pull to solve mysteries, sneaking around without getting caught, and doing something good for other people? Or do you feel the pull to relive your youth?"

Delphine frowned. "Sometimes you're really annoying, you know that?"

"Only because I am right."

She huffed. He was partially right, she'd give him that. She wasn't in her prime anymore, and sometimes she missed the past because back then, death had been more of an intellectual construct than an impending reality. But there were also things she didn't miss, and she did love her current life. Well, she enjoyed it, anyway.

"I have to do *something* though. I can't sit around and knit socks until the problem goes away and hope that the Falls clears my name. What if they're the very ones trying to implicate me?"

"It could be one individual working alone," said Kenji. "Maybe it's someone who has nothing to do with the Falls."

"Or someone who has nothing to do with the Falls anymore?" She narrowed her eyes at him.

"What are you saying?" he asked, sounding defensive.

Delphine looked away. "Nothing."

Kenji pursed his lips and went back to raking.

"One way or another, I have to get to the bottom of this before it's too late," she said.

Silence except for the metal tines of the rake scraping the pea gravel.

Delphine wanted to ask if he had any ideas, but knew he never revealed much without having concrete evidence, so it was useless to press him further. "Well, let me know if you come up with anything."

"I will."

"Kenji?"

"Yes, Delphine?"

"You wouldn't consider coming out of retirement and partnering with me on this, would you? They're going to find a way to take me down unless I find le Grande Fromage first. We could do it, you and I."

Kenji shook his head. "I'm sorry, but no. I am out of the business."

She figured he would decline. He didn't seem to miss their old life as much as she sometimes did.

"Don't you feel like you're too old to be getting back into that game?" he asked.

Delphine's brows rose at the frankness of his question. But she always appreciated his honest, if at times too unfiltered, thoughts. "I suppose. But right now, I don't seem to have a choice."

"I wish we had a regular retirement. More gardening, less espionage." He leaned on his rake again.

She smiled, almost getting lost in his grey eyes for a second time. This wouldn't do at all. There was no time for romance, real or imagined. Then she nodded at the pea gravel. "It looks like you're doing okay."

"I am trying," he said.

After a few beats of silence, she turned to leave.

"Delphine?" Kenji called after her.

"Yes?" she said, her voice higher than she would've liked.

"Be careful."

# CHAPTER 5

Delphine entered her house through the garage and went straight to the backyard to sit under the pergola. It was another beautiful morning—another perfect day to be outside. She checked her phone for messages, but there were none.

She needed to get moving. If she didn't, she could end up taking the fall for someone else's illicit activities. But whose?

Kenji was right. There were only a few possible reasons that someone might become desperate enough to take action: Love, sex, money, and power. Often they were so closely connected that it was impossible to tell them apart.

Maybe soaking her feet would be a good idea, she decided. That always felt so relaxing. Surely her granddaughter would approve of a foot soak. Since it used so much less water than a bath, it would be a good alternative, right? Well, what Zooey didn't know wouldn't hurt her this once. Delphine went inside and gathered a few supplies while a pot of water heated on the stove. She brought everything out to the patio, poured the hot water into a little plastic tub, and sat down again, waiting for the water to cool a bit.

Some days she did miss the action and fast pace of her former job, but this was not an ideal way to dip her toes back in those waters. It seemed as though she didn't have a choice now, however, so she might as well jump in with both feet. So to speak.

When the water in the tub had cooled to the perfect temperature, she added a little purple tablet that started to fizz as it sank. Her daughter-in-law Greta, Griffin's mom, had given her some lovely herbal soaks for Christmas that smelled of lavender and lemon. She carefully lowered her feet into the tub, sipped her tea, and thought some more.

She could probably manage the situation on her own, although that wasn't ideal. And as all agents had been taught, it was also discouraged.

Her mind wandered back to that time in Estonia, years and years ago, when the Falls had been asked to coordinate with local government to investigate alleged illegal logging operations in national parks. She had arrived in the country before Kenji, and in her youthful foolishness she decided to act on a tip—by herself. She posed as a hiker and made her way through the forest with the cover story that she'd been separated from her group. She'd found what looked like a logging encampment and settled into the brush to watch. She did see men cut down a few trees…

But the rest of what happened was rather unexpected. Once a tree was felled, four of the burly woodsmen sat down around the stump and began to play cards and drink something hot out of insulated carafes.

Delphine had been so enthralled that she lost track of her surroundings, and a group of the bearded, swarthy card players managed to sneak up on her. She barely managed to escape, thanks to being faster and more agile than her pursuers, but had to hide out in the forests along the northern shore of Lake Peipsi for two days before she could make it back to Kenji and the rest of their group, who had almost given up on her.

Eventually her team had managed to figure out the mystery of the illegal logging—it was in truth an illicit canasta betting ring with some illegal Chinese tea smuggling thrown in for good measure. But the most important thing to have come out of that mission for Delphine was the lesson to never go it alone.

And all that had been when she was young. Although still smart as a whip and able to kill someone with one hand, these days she was also quite aware that she was human, and one day her luck would run out.

Yes, it would be unwise to try anything on her own. And that meant she needed to find a partner, fast. But Delphine couldn't trust anyone. She thought she trusted Kenji, but he'd declined to get more involved. Why? Shouldn't he be the first in line to help keep her out of danger?

There was no way Kenji could be the Big Cheese. Or was there? Maybe that was why he refused to work with her. It made sense, on the surface. But if she spent too much time suspecting one of her best friends had tried to set her up … Well, that would be too much. No, she wouldn't go down that road.

Delphine shook her head and splashed her feet in the water with frustration. This would not do! The one person who had always had her back still had her back; she had to believe that was so.

She pushed her doubt away—for the time being, anyway—and let reason take its place. Kenji's stated reason for not teaming up with her was valid. They were retired, and it was time for a different, more peaceful life. He would help how he could, but not in the way she'd hoped.

Kenji was well connected in Los Angeles and might be able to dig up some information for her that she couldn't get herself. Often, his subtle approach was more productive than her direct tack. It was one reason they'd made such a good team when they were with the Falls.

She ran through the names of everyone else she could think of. Most people she knew these days were from the Falls or the Trotting Foxes. Some people belonged to both groups, so her list was shorter than she expected. And the list had one fatal flaw:

The people she trusted lacked experience, and the ones with experience, she didn't trust.

She wiggled her toes in the little tub. The fizz had fizzled and the water was tepid, and she still had a big problem. Who would she be able to call on? She didn't like admitting she needed someone, but oh well. Sometimes even an ex-agent needed help, plain and simple.

If there was no one suitable in her immediate circles, she would need to cast a wider net. Her mind drifted back to recent events and places she'd visited. She thought some more.

In the movies, you rarely saw anyone sitting around thinking. That was prime screen time, wasted. People wanted to see explosions, car chases, maybe a little romance. How much of that was real life? This was real life, thought Delphine. Soaking your feet, drinking tea, thinking.

By the time she'd gone back inside, fixed herself something to eat, and done the dishes, she had a plan. After putting the last dish away, Delphine picked up her phone and made a call.

# CHAPTER 6

The next day, Delphine stood at the American Airlines domestic baggage claim at LAX, waiting for an arriving passenger. She knew who she was looking for, but the traveler had no idea who he was looking for. He would recognize her though.

She checked the time on her phone. 11:40 a.m. Not bad, considering that only twenty-four hours earlier she'd come up with her plan and here she was, already getting help. She sent up a thank-you to the powers that be that she still had enough pull to get things to happen so quickly.

Yesterday afternoon Kenji had called to check on her, and she'd explained her idea to him.

"If you think that will work, it is worth trying," he'd told her.

"Are you sure you won't change your mind about partnering up?" she asked, trying to convince him one last time.

"I want to leave that life behind," he said.

"Even if that means more trouble for me?"

Kenji paused before answering. "I will be available in an unofficial support capacity."

"Hooray," Delphine said, turning her gaze skyward with sarcasm.

"I heard that," said Kenji, and Delphine stuck out her tongue. "That too."

She hadn't known what else to say. She knew her anger was more frustration than anything else; the whole situation was a bother that she'd rather not be bothered with.

"I *can't* do it, Delphine. Think about it."

Delphine had thought about it. Assuming he was not the Big Cheese, if he helped her, they might both end up implicated a big smelly mess, since he had been her partner. They could accuse him of being in on it, and the last thing she wanted to do was implicate her best friend. "Dammit, I guess you're right."

"Can I come over for dinner?" he had asked.

Now she was at the airport, waiting on a flight that had been delayed. She'd made better time getting across town than she'd anticipated, and had a few minutes to kill, which wasn't hard at the airport, if you enjoyed people watching. There didn't seem to be a way to outsmart the Los Angeles freeway system; she'd been trying for years. She pulled out her phone for something to do and noticed a reminder on the lock screen about picking up Zooey after school and watching her for a few hours until her father picked her up.

Heavens! She'd forgotten all about telling Sean earlier in the week that she would babysit. Now with everything else going on, she wasn't sure if she'd be able to make it back in time to get Zooey straight from school. Delphine dialed Marvis' number.

"Marv, can you do me a huge favor? Could you pick up Zooey at three thirty from school, maybe take her to the bookstore for a bit, and bring her by my place around five?"

She waited as Marvis checked her datebook. The woman didn't even sneeze without checking that planner of hers. Marvis came back on the line and confirmed she could help out.

"Oh, thank you so much," said Delphine. "I owe you one. Okay yes, I owe you another one. Gotta run. Thanks, dear!"

Zooey and Marvis would have a good time together; they always did on the rare occasions that Delphine had to offload her granddaughter due to more pressing obligations. But that wouldn't stop Zooey from giving her crap about going back on her word about their bookstore trip.

Passengers from the first Miami flight of the day began to trickle into the area and surround the baggage carousel. Delphine spotted him as soon as he stepped off the escalator. He looked wary, and she liked that. It was a good sign to be that cognizant of one's surroundings.

A group of tourists speaking Japanese huddled around a pillar, blocking her view of him as he came closer. She took a few steps to her left so he'd be able to see who was waiting for him.

When the man saw Delphine, he stopped dead in his tracks, surprise in his eyes. His backpack had been slung over one shoulder, but now fell off his arm and onto the ground. She hoped he didn't have a laptop in there.

Then his face showed fear, and finally anger. He looked back the way he'd come, perhaps debating whether he could make a run for it. In a way, she wouldn't blame him if he did, but she hoped he wouldn't. She didn't feel like chasing anyone through an airport today.

After another few seconds, his entire body seemed to deflate, and he reflected nothing but pure defeat.

The group of tourists had stopped talking and were watching the curious scene unfold. One of them took pictures with his phone, turning first to Delphine—*click-click-click*, then to her discombobulated counterpart—*click-click*.

One of the women in the cluster of people walked up to the man as he stood and stared at his backpack. "Excuse me," she said with a bow. "Are you movie star?"

The man opened his mouth, but no words came out.

Why didn't anyone think *she* was a movie star? wondered Delphine. It was certainly more plausible than her guest being one. Although he was rather handsome, it was true.

After a few seconds, the tourist turned to face Delphine. "Are *you* film star?"

Delphine felt vindicated for a second before giving the woman a polite smile and saying, "No dear, and please tell your friend to stop taking pictures of us, or I'll have to confiscate his phone and run over it with my car."

The tourist's eyes went wide, and she hurried back to her group, where she spoke in rapid Japanese, presumably relaying Delphine's message. They all gawked at her for a moment, then turned as a unit to give her their backs.

The man picked up his backpack and walked her direction her at a snail's pace, looking like a disappointed third grader.

Delphine put on her best welcome-to-LA face and extended her hand. "Detective Magnusson. How wonderful to see you again."

# CHAPTER 7

Detective Roland Magnusson of the Largo, Florida Police Department looked at Delphine's extended hand. His first reaction was to skip the formal greeting and make a beeline for the exit, take the stairs two at a time up to the departure level, and purchase a return ticket home, no matter the cost. However, he knew Delphine possessed mysterious and far-reaching powers, and there was nowhere to hide. He took her hand with reluctance and shook it without much enthusiasm.

"What in the name of all that is holy am I doing here?" he asked.

Delphine's eyes darted around the baggage claim area. She took him by the elbow and led him toward the growing group of people waiting at the baggage carousel.

"I know I owe you an explanation, but let's collect your things and I'll tell you once we're underway in the car," she said.

"I don't like this," he said as they stood beside the carousel, his backpack straps still trailing along the floor.

"Me neither," she said. "We have no cover here."

"No, I mean … What? Are you being followed?" He wondered what he had just walked into. Were they in danger? He scanned the room but wasn't sure what he was looking for.

"No, I don't like those buzzers that alert you the carousel is about to start. We were standing right under the speaker."

"Are you being serious right now?" he asked, angry at himself for believing something was really wrong. Delphine lifted one shoulder but remained quiet.

His boss, Captain Perez, hadn't said much when he'd called Roland at home to tell him that he was to leave immediately for Los Angeles, and to take his service weapon—hence the checked bag. His partner Rojas joked that he was going to be assigned to protect a supermodel on a beach photo shoot and told him to send pictures. His wife Christina had told him not to leave his clothes in the dryer when he left.

Now as he stood at a baggage carousel at LAX, surrounded by a sea of well-dressed people who all seemed to be on their phones talking to their agents, his anger grew. He looked at Delphine, who stared with trepidation at the overhead speaker. *Her.* The woman who had ruined his case against the ring of senior jewel thieves he'd exposed last month. She had ruined everything when she went over his head to pull some strings to get one of the women released. Just because that woman was the other grandma of Delphine's favorite granddaughter, Griffin.

So what that he might not have cracked the case as fast without Delphine and Griffin's help? So what that Griffin was nice, and cute too, and he still thought of her from time to time? Delphine had encroached on his case and his life and yes, he still held a grudge. And he didn't care if that wasn't considered "healthy mental behavior," or whatever the self-help gurus called it.

Here he was, clear on the other side of the country with no idea what he was supposed to be doing other than indulging the whims of a woman who should knitting sweaters for her grandkids.

The overhead buzzer blared (she'd been right, it was a lot louder than it needed to be). The machinery started up, and everyone moved closer to the edge of the plate carousel as if the game of getting one's bag first was an Olympic sport. Californians were so competitive, thought Roland. Nonetheless, as soon as he identified his suitcase when it slid down the chute and hit the metal guard rail with a muffled *bang!* he muscled his way forward and grabbed it before it made it three feet around the carousel.

The group of Japanese tourists were still waiting for their luggage, and the woman who had asked him if he was an actor was watching his every move. Roland pulled his sunglasses out of his jacket pocket, slid them on his face, and gave the woman his best attempt at a lopsided movie-star smile. She gasped and tugged at the sleeve of the woman next to her, but to no avail. Roland and Delphine left the building without fanfare.

When they got to her vehicle, he almost dropped his backpack again. "What is it with you ladies and German cars?" he asked. Delphine's Mercedes wasn't as nice as Marge Flanders' had been —that one was way over the top. Come to think of it, Marge had been way over the top too.

This car was stunning, nonetheless. The deep, midnight-blue color hinted at the luxury waiting within.

"At my age, you want a little bling," she said, popping the trunk.

"I thought we agreed not to use that word."

"Right, sorry."

Roland retrieved his weapon from his suitcase and placed the bag in the back. "Your trunk smells weird," he said. No explanation was given by his host.

They got in the car, exited the parking structure, and began making their way out of the airport at glacial speed due to traffic. Still she said nothing.

"So?" he asked.

"Sew buttons?" she responded.

"What? Forget it. Seriously though," he said. "You need to tell me what's happening. Had I known it was *you* I was meeting, I never would have agreed to this." He put the heels of his hands over his eyes and rubbed.

"It's sweet how you think you had a choice in the matter," she said.

Roland felt his blood pressure rise. Hopefully he'd be able to get home before this woman caused him any serious health issues. He couldn't believe the nerve she had, going over his head—nor the fact that his captain hadn't told him a thing. Rogelio Perez would be getting an earful from Roland Magnusson as soon as he had a moment to himself to place a call. "I guess you instructed my bosses not to tell me anything."

"I was under no obligation to tell them anything. They know as much as you do."

His hands shot away from his face. "You can't go around hijacking people!"

"Well," said Delphine, merging onto the freeway, "it seems that I can."

They drove in silence for a few minutes and Roland looked out the window. As they left the area around the airport, all he saw was brown sky, traffic, and palm trees. He'd been to Southern California only twice before in his life—once when he was about fourteen, when his family went to Disneyland and Universal Studios, and once for some detective training about five years ago. On the first occasion he'd been too young to care much about the city, and on the second there hadn't been a chance to look around.

"The last time we saw each other, I told you I never wanted to see you again," he said.

"No, you told me you didn't want to see me in Miami again." She kept her eyes on the road. "Roland—"

"You can call me Detective Magnusson."

"Roland, let me be frank with you."

Roland snorted.

"Let me be frank with you," she started again, sounding more annoyed. "I'm in some trouble. I need someone I can trust. My life may depend on it. Despite what you might think, I was very impressed by how you handled the Blingsters'—I mean Marge's

—case. Even though, for some reason, you don't seem to like me much."

Roland snorted again.

"But you're smart, impartial, and not local. Those are all tremendous advantages. In short, I need your help," said Delphine.

Roland said nothing and continued to stare out the window. She did sound sincere, he had to give her that. He also knew that first impressions could be deceiving and was therefore still undecided about what to think. But he was curious.

The landscape began to change to taller buildings and the freeway became even more congested.

"Are you going to give me any details?" he asked. "I can't do much if I don't know why the hell I'm here."

Delphine gave him a stern look, which he took to mean she wasn't a fan of cursing. Well, that was too bad for her.

"Fine," she said, adjusting her grip on the steering wheel. "I did pull a few strings and told your superiors that I required your assistance for an unknown period of time to work with me on an important investigation. National security is at stake, I told them."

"Is that true?"

Delphine tilted her head. "Yes and no," she said.

Roland stared at her, waiting for her to continue.

"Yes, if you eat cheese. No, if you're lactose intolerant or vegan."

That explanation was about as clear as the air quality in the Los Angeles basin, thought Roland. "I guess I'm going to have to expect a lot more unhelpful answers from you," he said.

"For now," she said, and they drove on in silence.

# CHAPTER 8

An hour-and-a-half later, Delphine pulled her Mercedes into the Big Bob parking lot in Burbank and shook her head at Kenji's restaurant choice. Leave it to him to want to meet at a burger joint.

Roland slung his backpack over his shoulder, and she put her purse under her arm, and they walked into the diner. Within minutes, they sat at a circular booth in the far corner of the main room, Delphine in the middle and Roland on one side. Menus and water glasses had appeared, and now all they needed was Kenji. Delphine had texted him when they were within twenty minutes of the restaurant, but traffic was heavy everywhere and he was probably stuck somewhere between Burbank and Pasadena, just like they had been delayed as they'd driven from West LA. They could be in for a long wait.

"Aren't you going to ask why we're here?" said Delphine.

"You mean other than getting something to eat?" Roland asked, and she nodded. "I gave up trying to figure out what's going on about an hour ago. What's good?" He began looking over the lunch choices, squinting at the restaurant's logo in the upper right-hand corner of the menu—a plus-sized kid wearing blue and white checkered overalls who looked ecstatic to be holding a plate with a giant burger on it.

"Nothing," said Delphine.

The restaurant chain was a Southern California institution, but that didn't mean Delphine wanted to eat their food. Memories flashed through her mind of bringing her children, Sean and Greta, here for hamburgers and shakes when they were little. The kids loved the place, but it had never been her cup of tea. Everything seemed so greasy—even the salads, which should not be possible.

"What can I get you two?" asked their server as the young man placed two glasses of water on the table. Delphine noted that he never looked at her or Roland, and instead kept his eyes on the table and then the wall behind the booth.

Roland scanned the menu again. "I'll have—"

"We're waiting on someone," interrupted Delphine. Roland looked surprised to hear it, and she knew it was time to start explaining.

The server swung his head to try and flip his long bangs out of his eyes. "Okay. Would your son like a coloring page and some crayons while you wait?"

"Would you like to keep your spleen?" snapped Roland.

"I'll take that as a no," said the young man, unfazed, and wandered away from their table.

"That was sweet," said Delphine. Roland turned red, but whether from anger or embarrassment she wasn't sure. She found it endearing, even though she knew he was equally as mad at her as he was at the young server.

"Can you get to the point already?" said Roland. "You need my help with something. What is it?"

Delphine got out her phone and stared at it, pretending to check her text messages. Even though she had gone through all the effort of getting Roland to LA to partner with her on this problem that could have serious ramifications on the quality of the remainder of her life, she still felt a little silly explaining how she found smelly French cheese in the trunk of her car. But she needed to get it over with.

She put her phone away and said, "All right. Where was I?"

"Nowhere," said Roland, who had gone back to studying the menu.

Delphine closed her eyes and rubbed the bridge of her nose.

"Delphine needs your help with an old case," said a third voice.

When Roland and Delphine looked up, Kenji sat at the edge of the booth.

"You got here fast," she said.

"I know a back way." Kenji scooched closer to her along the vinyl bench. He frowned and moved away again.

"What are you doing?" Delphine asked.

"Couldn't you get a rectangular table? No matter where I sit, I can't see you." He scooched away from her some more until he was almost falling out of the booth.

Delphine smiled. It was a known fact that men liked to be seated across from the person they were talking to, while women preferred to sit next to their confidant. A handy fact that had served her well on countless occasions, on the job and off. At least he was sitting across from Roland.

"Next time," she said. "This was where they stuck us today. And I don't see why we couldn't meet in my kitchen. You live right across the street, for heaven's sake." She slid her menu over to him and he used both hands to arrange it on the tabletop until it was centered directly in front of the Yale logo on the front of his sweatshirt.

"Yes, but you don't make burgers like these," he said, stabbing the plastic menu with his index finger. It landed on something called "The Big Bob Combo." It looked about as appetizing as a used oil filter from a 1965 Dodge station wagon.

"Roland, this is Kenji Yamamoto, my former partner. Kenji, this is Detective Roland Magnusson, on special assignment from the Largo Police in Florida."

"Okay," said Kenji, nonplussed.

"Hello," said Roland, also nonplussed.

Delphine knew then and there she had made the right decision in bringing Roland to LA. They would all work together just fine.

The server meandered back over, and they all ordered. Kenji got his Big Bob Combo, Delphine ordered a salad, and Roland chose a plant-based burger with a side salad instead of fries. Delphine wanted to ask the server for a few crayons for her two sons, but decided against it.

"Do you not eat meat?" Kenji asked Roland.

"My wife has decided we're vegetarian," Roland said.

"I'm guessing that is a new development in your relationship," said Kenji.

Roland looked confused. "What makes you think that?"

"No reason," said Kenji.

"He does that all the time," Delphine told Roland.

"What, put people off?"

"No, make freakishly accurate observations without telling you how he comes to his conclusions," she explained.

"Great," said Roland, "that's fun."

"He's right though, isn't he?" she asked.

Roland looked at her and took another drink of water. Then he said, "So when you say you two used to be partners, is that your way of saying you used to be boyfriend-girlfriend?"

Kenji's body shook with a silent laugh, and he looked at Delphine. "Where did you find this guy?"

"What's that mean?" asked Roland, sounding indignant.

"Settle down, kids," said Delphine. "And let me explain. Roland, Kenji and I used to work for a shadow agency called the Falls."

"Never heard of it," he said.

Delphine said, "That's how we operate."

"You said 'we' instead of 'they'," observed Kenji.

She said, "Slip of the tongue, I guess." It had felt natural to speak like she still worked there, and that was a little worrying.

Roland put his elbows on the table and leaned in toward

Delphine. "How do I know this group exists? You could be making all this bull—baloney up."

"It's not like they give us mugs with our—I mean their—logo on them, Roland," she said.

"I would love a T-shirt though," said Kenji.

Roland tried again. "I want proof."

"The woman made one phone call, and within twenty-four hours you're all the way across the country sitting in one of the best diners in California. Isn't that proof enough?" asked Kenji. "You should get a milkshake, by the way. They are the best."

Delphine looked at Roland and held an open palm in Kenji's direction. "What he said. Except not about the milkshakes. Those things taste like bilge water."

Roland smiled at that, but Delphine wasn't sure why. She'd been serious.

"Don't listen to her," said Kenji.

"Can someone please circle back to the point?" asked Roland.

By that point, Delphine had studied the detective enough to realize he was on the verge of another outburst that would most likely contain profanity. "Before you ask a million more questions," she said, "the only thing I can tell you right now is that the name comes from a significant landmark near the main headquarters, and more than one government is involved. Most of the time. Sort of. It's quite nebulous, really."

"And if you told me any more about it, you'd have to kill me," said Roland with a smirk.

"Correct," said Delphine, and Roland's smirk faded.

"Technically I'm retired, but the contacts I've made over the years keep coming in handy."

"You're retired too?" Roland asked Kenji.

"Yes," said Kenji. He leaned in closer and added, "But just when you think you are out, they pull you back in."

"Ah," said Roland, nodding with understanding.

Delphine rolled her eyes. For men, at least 90 percent of life could be summed up by a *Godfather* quote.

"Okay," said Roland. "But none of that explains why I'm here."

"I was getting to that part," said Delphine. "Kenji, what have you found out?

"Not much," he said.

Delphine leaned back in the booth and crossed her arms. "You could have told us that in a text."

"There are no burgers in text messages."

"Fine." She proceeded to tell Roland the basics of the original Big Cheese operation: their objective, the unsolved case of Simon Pegbottam's murder, and the suspiciously quick conclusion of the entire operation.

Roland listened and nodded several times but said nothing.

"Then the other night, I found four wheels of imported cheese in the trunk of my car. Our former manager Richard Dere happened to be there. Coincidence? I don't think so. Now he's investigating me. He thinks I could be the Big Cheese."

"That must have been what I smelled in your trunk when I put my suitcase back there," said Roland. "I hope my shorts don't smell like cheese now."

"We have these things out here in California called washing machines," said Delphine.

"He has a point though," agreed Kenji. "Food smells can be an issue. I had to throw away a brand-new pair of jeans while we were working on that onion heist."

Delphine looked at Kenji for a second, willing him to stop sharing top-secret information, then resumed speaking. "The bigger issue here is that I'm innocent. But if they successfully frame me for bringing these cheeses into the country without paying the tariff, Richard will try to connect me to the old case. And perhaps also Peggbottam's murder."

The server came and placed their food on the table.

"Thank you!" said Kenji as he tucked his napkin into the top of his sweatshirt collar and prepared to dig in. He slid a folded piece of paper across the table to Delphine with one hand while he picked up a French fry with the other.

Delphine took the paper and held it under the table, where she unfolded it and surveyed the message—a street address written in Kenji's precise hand, followed by a series of numbers and letters: *SS, 2D, 3L, S3, DD*. No name, no phone number. "This is someplace downtown."

"Let me see," said Roland, and she handed him the paper under the table. He looked at the message, refolded the paper, and slid it back across the tabletop to her, refocusing on his burger. If he was curious about the code, he didn't let it show.

"You called Judy," said Delphine.

"Yes," said Kenji with a mouthful of food.

A hint of a twinge of jealousy ran down her spine, even though there was no reason for it. To her knowledge Kenji had never been romantically interested in Judy, and even if he did feel that way, it was none of her business. He was only a friend now. And she was glad that he'd called her. Perhaps this information was what Judy had wanted to tell her the day before at the Falls office but couldn't.

"Judy is Richard's assistant," Kenji said, looking at Roland. "She was not able to shed much light on anything but did provide that information as a starting point."

Delphine tapped the edge of the folded piece of paper on the table. "I wonder how she got this."

"Not my place to ask," said Kenji. "Besides, does it matter?"

"It very well might!" said Delphine, almost indignant that Kenji would ask such a thing. "She does work for Richard."

"It could be a setup," agreed Roland. He put a forkful of salad in his mouth and looked at Kenji's plate, covered in steak fries. "You're not going to eat all of those," he said, partly as a question, mostly as a declaration.

Kenji looked up at him and once he figured out what Roland wanted, gestured his approval and Roland swooped in for a few fries.

"He's right, Kenji," said Delphine.

"Yes," said Kenji. "I hadn't thought of that." He took another bite of food and looked at her with narrowed eyes while he chewed.

"What?" she asked.

"I don't like any of this."

"There's nothing to like," said Delphine, letting her mind wander back in time to the original Big Cheese days. There had to be something from back then that could shed light on what was going on now.

They ate in silence for a while, until Kenji did everyone at the table a huge favor and broke the tension by asking Roland a few questions about his work in Florida. Roland seemed grateful for the diversion, and told them about his partner and their captain, and a few hazy details about a case involving a politician and a stolen dolphin.

By the time Roland and Kenji had finished their burgers, they were talking about sports of some kind. Delphine wasn't sure which one; they were all the same, after all.

"You haven't touched your salad." Kenji pointed to Delphine's plate.

"I wouldn't eat a saltine from this place," she said, pushing her full bowl toward the edge of the table.

"Do you guys want any dessert?" asked their server, who had walked up to the booth. He jerked his head in another unsuccessful attempt to remove his hair from his face as he looked at Delphine. "We have junior-sized shakes and sundaes for your kids."

"I will take an adult-sized chocolate shake to go," said Kenji, not looking up from polishing off his last fry.

Roland, however, glared at the server. "You need a haircut."

The kid either ignored Roland or didn't hear him—it was hard to tell.

"Nothing for me, thank you," said Delphine.

When it came time to pay, she picked up the tab and they walked out to the parking lot together.

"You will want to go to that address tomorrow, sometime between the hours of ten and three," said Kenji. He hit a button on the remote on his keychain and the electric Volvo SUV right next to Delphine's Mercedes chirped. "And yes, Delphine, it's exactly what you think it is."

She unlocked her own car. "Anything else I should know?"

Kenji slid into the driver's seat of the Volvo. "Kraft Parmesan," he said before closing the door.

"Any idea what that meant?" asked Roland.

"Not a clue," said Delphine.

# CHAPTER 9

"We can't do anything with the information from Kenji yet," said Delphine.

They were parked in traffic on one of the many ubiquitous Los Angeles freeways. At least they all seemed the same to Roland. Surely the locals could tell them apart, but all he saw everywhere they went were cars, cars, and more cars. The last sign they passed had indicated they were on the 134, but it was meaningless information to him.

"What was that writing on the paper Kenji gave you?" he asked.

"Instructions on how to get into a secret cheese marketplace. I did a little research when you and Kenji were talking about golf."

"We were talking about baseball," said Roland.

"Anyway," said Delphine. "The UCC is underneath the Grand Central Market downtown. They're closed now. We have to wait until tomorrow to check it out."

"What's UCC stand for?"

"Underground Cheese Consortium."

"Ah," said Roland, trying to sound like that explained everything. It didn't, but the important part was that they'd have to wait till tomorrow to do anything. "Sounds like I've got the rest of today off then." He adjusted the passenger seat to lean back farther and interlaced his fingers behind his head. Perfect—he could use a minute to collect himself. And call his boss to complain.

"No time off. We have plans for the rest of the day. I don't think there is an immediate threat, but we also don't have time to waste. Plus, I have some prior commitments to take care of."

"Oh." A sense of duty replaced his momentary disappointment at not getting a break. Regardless of how badly he'd been duped, he was still on the job. And she'd just bought him a vegan burger that hadn't been too bad. "Where are we headed now?"

"To the CalCreative Charter Elementary School," said Delphine.

"You don't think we should at least maybe try a middle school instead?"

"We are not going there to look for cheese smugglers, we are picking up my granddaughter. Fortunately, we got out of that ridiculous restaurant earlier than I thought we would, and while you were ogling that Bentley a few minutes ago, I texted my friend Marvis to let her know she's off the hook for babysitting duties."

Roland only half heard what Delphine said, since he was still thinking about the Bentley. He sighed.

"Honestly, don't you get enough of that type of gross display of wealth in Florida?" Delphine asked him, irritated by his daydreaming.

"Yes," said Roland. "But I wasn't ogling the car, I was ogling the woman inside the car."

"Oh for Pete's sake."

"These California women are so healthy," said Roland in an incredulous tone. "West Coast healthy is different than Miami healthy. Yes, there's a difference and no, I'm not going to explain it to you."

"I had no intention of asking you to," said Delphine.

Roland thought about the woman in the Bentley, sitting in the back seat with the window down. She'd been blond of course, but had a more natural beauty than he'd expected, and when she smiled at him, he had the presence of mind to smile back. It had been harmless. A moment akin to the scene in *American Graffiti*, when Richard Dreyfuss spotted Suzanne Somers in the back of that T-Bird. Only in the movie, Dreyfuss went off to college the next day, while Roland was to report for babysitting duty. Also in Roland's version, the beautiful blond woman peered at the elderly lady who was driving him down the 134 freeway, laughed, and rolled the window back up.

Delphine got off the freeway, and a few minutes later they drove up to a school that seemed to be housed in a renovated industrial building, with attached structures made out of shipping containers. No way it could be a school, Roland thought.

"Wait," he said, now realizing he must have missed something earlier. "Did you say babysitting duties?"

Delphine made a frustrated huffing sound but didn't say anything.

They took their place in a line of Teslas, Land Rovers, and BMWs parked along the curb outside the industrial park that might be a school, and sure enough, a few minutes later a stream of children emerged from the front doors of the warehouse. Must have been some kind of special school for kids who needed extra attention, Roland surmised. Normal kids went to normal schools in normal buildings.

Delphine inched her way to the front of the line, where a small girl with shoulder-length brown hair and a backpack as big as she was bounced to the car on the balls of her feet and got into the back seat.

"Hello, Zooey," said Delphine as she pulled the car away from the curb.

"Hello, Delphine," the girl said.

Roland turned to look at the child, who was buckling herself into a car seat he hadn't noticed before. He had a question that he figured he'd probably regret asking, but he couldn't help himself. "Don't you have to help buckle her in?" he asked Delphine.

Delphine started to answer, but her granddaughter interrupted.

"I've got this," announced Zooey.

"You heard her," said Delphine.

Roland went back to staring straight ahead, wondering why he had bothered.

"Grandma, who is the miscreant in the passenger seat?" asked Zooey.

His head whipped around so fast that the little girl jumped. "If someone in this car is a miscreant, it's not me."

"Roland, stop trying to be scary," said Delphine.

"Yeah Roland, stop it. I don't find him the least bit scary, Grandma," said Zooey.

"How old is she?" Roland asked Delphine.

Before Delphine could answer, Zooey said, "I'm eight, but very mature for my age."

"Okay," said Roland.

"Zooey, this is my friend Detective Magnusson," said Delphine. "But you can call him Roland."

"Hi, Rolly," said Zooey.

Roland turned in his seat again. "No, that's not my name. It's—"

"Rolly Polly, Rolly Polly," sang Zooey.

"That's not even how you pronounce roly poly," said Roland.

"Rolly Polly."

"But it's—"

"Rolly Polly, Rolly Polly!"

Delphine drove them to a bookstore and coffee shop in a neighborhood called Atwater. Zooey ordered herself a vegan hot chocolate (almond milk and special marshmallows, she explained). They walked around the store together, looking at all the different kinds of books.

Zooey continued to sing her favorite new song, and Roland

was about to lose it. Delphine must have finally taken pity on him because she made a half-hearted attempt to intervene. "Zooey dear, stop calling him that."

"Yeah, or I'll arrest you," said Roland. "I'm a police detective, remember."

Zooey stopped her dancing in the main aisle and looked at Roland. "My daddy always says he's going to arrest me when I do things he doesn't like," she says. "But he never does." And she skipped away to the children's section, singing her song.

"I assume her dad is in law enforcement?" said Roland.

Delphine shrugged. "Sort of. This line of work is a family business."

Roland and Delphine continued to walk the main aisle, and they could hear Zooey in the back of the store.

"Rolly Rolly Rolly," she sang.

Roland looked at Delphine. "Is she ever going to stop?" he asked.

"Probably not," said Delphine. "Don't you like it? You didn't seem to mind when Griffin called you that."

"Totally different. She didn't do it every five seconds. And Griffin was cuter."

Delphine smiled.

"I mean, it was just less annoying when she did it."

A few minutes later they found Zooey, looking at a book about someone called Enola Holmes, still singing absently.

"Zooey," Roland said. "I have asked nicely several times. Is there anything I can do to get you to stop calling me that?" he asked her.

Her eyes gazed skyward and her mouth squished to one side as she thought about it. "Probably not," she finally said. "But your best bet would be to buy me a book. That has a 56 percent chance of working."

"Please stop blackmailing your elders, dear. I've told you, that's not very nice behavior," Delphine said.

"Wait a minute," Roland said to Delphine. "If that's my best shot, I'm willing to pay her ransom."

Zooey chose the Enola Holmes book, Roland bought it, and she was quiet all the way back to Delphine's house.

Delphine parked in the driveway, and when they got out of the car, Roland went to the back and lifted his suitcase out of the already open trunk, resting it on the threshold. Then he leaned in and sniffed the fabric of the bag. He definitely smelled cheese, but couldn't tell if it came from the trunk or the suitcase. He looked up to find Zooey staring at him, open-mouthed.

"It smells funny," he explained to her with a weak smile.

Zooey scooped up her grandmother's hand, and the two of them walked to the front door. "He's weird," she told her grandmother.

Delphine looked back and gave Roland a sly smile as he rolled his suitcase behind him and followed them inside.

After Zooey did some homework, the three of them made dinner together. Roland had not expected to have to participate, but both Zooey and Delphine were adamant. His wife never forced him to cook, since she knew he was about as proficient in the kitchen as an eight-year-old. But in this case, Zooey easily outdid him with her culinary skills.

When Delphine instructed Zooey to set the table, the girl decided that the moratorium on singing her favorite new song was over, and she started up with "Rolly Polly" again. He tried again to get her to stop, but she did not relent. He had to admire her perseverance though. A few times over the years he'd felt the stirrings of parental instincts, and Christina must have also, as she brought up the idea of having kids about once a year, usually around her birthday. But so far they'd not done anything about it, and today Roland was glad.

They sat down to dinner, Delphine at the head of the table, Zooey and Roland facing each other. A big platter of steaming mushroom bourguignon sat before them. It smelled delicious, and Roland couldn't wait to try it. He'd told Delphine that they didn't have to cook vegetarian on his account, but she insisted it was all Zooey's doing.

"I am morally and ethically against eating meat," the young girl informed him once they were seated.

Roland stayed quiet, unsure of what to say to a statement like that. It seemed best not to open that can of vegan worms. He reached out a hand toward the serving spoon but was stopped short by Delphine's voice.

"Zooey, would you like to say grace?"

"Okay grandma, but let's not call it grace."

Delphine shrugged. "All right."

"What do you call it?" Roland asked Zooey as his stomach growled.

"A somber moment of reflection and gratitude before partaking in our evening meal."

"Please begin, dear," said Delphine before Roland had a chance to laugh. The kid was a hoot when she wasn't being annoying.

Zooey looked at him but remained silent, and he realized she was waiting for him to bow his head. He dropped his gaze to his lap and prayed the whole thing wouldn't take too long.

"In the grand scheme of existence," began Zooey, "we gather here to share a meal. We honor the circle of life that brought us this food and the labor of those who made it possible. This meal symbolizes not just sustenance but a celebration of our interconnectedness. May every bite deepen our appreciation for life and strengthen our bonds. Let's celebrate existence by chowing down."

Roland looked at Delphine in confusion. Was this eight-year-old child for real? Delphine ignored his look, took the serving spoon, and served herself some mushroom bourguignon. He let Zooey go next, and then scooped a heaping serving onto his own plate.

"Don't forget the broccoli," said Zooey.

"I wouldn't dream of it," said Roland, reaching for the bowl of fresh steaming vegetables.

After a few minutes of eating in silence, the sporadic conversation centered around what Zooey was studying in school (Indigenous Art History and Math as an Abstract Concept were favorites, Intro to Currency Trading not so much). School had changed a lot since he was a kid, thought Roland.

As soon as they finished their meal, Delphine's son Sean arrived to take Zooey home.

Delphine introduced Roland to Sean as Zooey gathered her backpack and her new book.

"Mom, are you sure you want to have someone you hardly know in your house after dark?" Sean asked Delphine as he eyed Roland with suspicion.

"I'm not even going to dignify that with an answer," said Delphine. She looked at Roland, who also had no intention of responding. "Honestly. You turn seventy and suddenly your children think they're your parents."

Roland still kept his mouth shut.

Zooey ran up to her grandma, hugged her goodbye, and sang, "Bye, Rolly Polly!" all the way out the door.

Sean gave his mother one last disapproving look, went out the door, and closed it behind him.

"Kids can be so annoying, even if they are top-notch operatives," said Delphine as she and Roland walked into the kitchen. "Just think what he would have done if he knew you were spending the night."

"You're not taking me to a hotel?" asked Roland, surprised by her statement.

"No, you're staying in my guest room. That's why I had you bring your bag inside. This way, we can work together more closely."

Roland crossed his arms. "And I'm sure it has nothing to do with having me around for protection."

"Absolutely not. This is for convenience only."

"Great," said Roland, feeling more claustrophobic by the second. He collapsed onto the couch and looked around for the remote. It had been a very long, surprising, tiring, and somewhat disappointing day. And that Zooey had worn him out! He was going to watch TV, whether Delphine felt like it or not. "What streaming services do you have?"

"A few," said Delphine. "But there's no time for that. Go and get changed, we have to be at the dance studio by seven."

# CHAPTER 10

"Please tell me this has something to do with the case," said Roland as they drove through the Pasadena streets on their way to the Sassy Steppers Dance Studio.

"Of course it does," said Delphine. She eyed her fidgeting passenger. "I do wish you'd brought a nicer change of clothes."

Roland looked down at his plaid button-up shirt and jeans. "No one told me I'd be going to a black-tie event," he said. "Besides, it's just a dance studio, so what's the big deal?"

Delphine frowned. Kids today had no sense of propriety. Flip-flops to church, pajamas to the grocery store. It was terrible. "A good agent should be prepared for anything, and that includes always bringing a set of dress clothes on assignment."

"I'll remember that next time someone kidnaps me for work."

"What did you think of Zooey?" asked Delphine.

Roland paused before answering with a question of his own. "What's her deal?"

"I'm not sure what you mean, but if you're referring to her high IQ and advanced language and math skills, we prefer to call her gifted." Delphine hated putting any sort of label on people, especially children, but she also knew it was human nature. Labels helped people make sense of the world around them. It was when people stuck too rigidly to those categories that the trouble began.

Delphine found an open spot in front of the ScriptDoctor storefront and pulled in. "She reminds me so much of Griffin when she was that age." She watched Roland's face as she spoke, hoping to get a reaction from him at the mention of her other granddaughter's name. She thought she'd seen a flicker of interest when her name had come up before and wanted to try again. "A little awkward, but charming. And kind."

"She was cute," said Roland. "Zooey, I mean. But I think I get adults more than I do kids."

"Hmm," she said. Delphine hoped it was truly children he didn't understand and not women that he was clueless about. And this time he hadn't reacted at all to the mention of Griffin's name. Delphine was a tiny bit disappointed, as she'd sworn there had been some chemistry between them in Miami. Yes, Roland was married, and so was Griffin, technically—although she'd just filed for divorce from her loser husband. But that didn't mean something couldn't happen someday. Delphine knew about the slow burn, and she was in favor of it.

They sat and watched a dejected-looking Millennial trudge up to the ScriptDoctor door and pull on it with the hand that wasn't holding a giant Starbucks drink. The door wouldn't open, and the girl peered in and waved at someone inside.

"The California dream," said Roland.

"Sure," said Delphine.

"Do you think those places work? Because I have an idea for a movie about a detective who can talk to dead people."

Delphine raised a hand, hoping he would stop talking. "Let's go inside," she suggested.

"Okay," said Roland, and they got out of the car. "You look nice," he said as they walked to the studio.

Delphine smoothed the fabric of her burgundy-colored dress. It was one of her favorites. "Thank you."

"I'm still going to tell you more about my movie idea later," said Roland. "Hey, do you know any famous directors?"

Delphine smiled at that. She did know several, and also a few A-list actors and producers. Pedro Bernal crossed her mind again and her face flushed. "No."

They entered the studio and stood right inside the doors, where Delphine pointed out a few people to Roland.

"There's my friend Marvis, coming this way. Her husband Franko is over there, talking to…"

"Humpty Dumpty and one of the king's golf buddies?" asked Roland.

"The one who looks like Humpty Dumpty is Richard Dere. He runs the local Falls office and was my former boss. He's the one who questioned me two days ago. His golf buddy is Walter Shipley, whom we call Ship. Also a former agent like Kenji and myself."

"Got it," said Roland.

The three men stood in a line, shoulder to shoulder. Their arms were crossed and they rocked from their heels to the balls of their feet as they chatted over an Artie Shaw tune playing low in the background.

"Interesting," said Delphine, thinking aloud.

"What?" asked Roland.

"Oh. It's just that Richard has never come here before this week, and now he seems to be here all the time."

"Not a coincidence then."

"I don't think so."

By that point Marvis had made her way across the studio and walked up to them. She took Delphine's arm and Roland followed the two ladies to the back of the room where the refreshment table was set up. The main dance music hadn't started yet, but there were plenty of couples milling around the floor, waiting and warming up with arm circles and half-hearted forward folds. The place was surprisingly full, which was good for business. Perhaps now the Trotting Foxes could afford something better than tropical punch that had been banned in the EU.

"Is everything okay?" Marvis asked once they'd made their way through the crowd. "I got your message but wasn't sure what it meant."

"The less you know, the better," said Delphine. "But I do need your help."

"Anything for you, dear. But first … Hi there, I'm Marvis." She smiled and sidled closer to Roland, extending her arm to him.

"Hello," said Roland. He shook her hand and smiled back.

"Oh my," said Marvis. "That's quite a grip."

Delphine wondered if he had such a mesmerizing effect on all women, or just the ones she happened to know. She hoped it would end up being a boon, and not an inconvenience to her objectives. Nonetheless, she was impressed by his ability to adapt to all situations.

Roland managed to free himself from Marvis' clutches, and she elbowed Delphine and said, "Have you been holding out on me all this time?"

"Marvis, this is Roland. He's my brother's cousin's uncle, visiting from Florida. Roland, meet Marvis Schlott, one of my dear friends and your dance instructor for the evening."

"Ooo!" cooed Marvis. "It's my lucky night!"

"Excuse me?" said Roland.

"You are getting dance lessons tonight," Delphine informed him.

"Okay," said Roland. "Do they serve beer here?"

Marvis frowned. "No alcohol. We have some hazardous chemicals masquerading as fruit punch, but that's about it."

Roland looked disappointed. "I'll pass."

"Let's go, you tall thing you," said Marvis, tugging on his shirtsleeve.

But Delphine pulled his other shirtsleeve harder, and he leaned in toward her. "She doesn't know everything about my previous career," she said.

"That you worked for a secret agency?" he asked in a not-so-quiet voice.

Hush!" she scolded. "She also doesn't know that I sometimes killed people for a living. So don't spill the beans. Just pay attention to the room and keep an eye on me."

Roland nodded and let himself be led onto the dance floor. "Who says 'spill the beans' anymore?" he called back to her right before he was swallowed by a crowd of dancers.

Delphine placed herself next to the wall and stayed in the shadows as she surveyed the entire room. Her eyesight was still excellent, thank goodness. Scanning the space, nothing seemed out of the ordinary, and she hoped it stayed that way.

Delphine had brought her gun of course, like she always did, but she'd Roland to leave his at her house. She made it a rule to leave espionage and spying behind when she went dancing, and up until this week, that hadn't been a problem. She was retired after all, and the only other person who knew her real profession was Ship. Their unspoken agreement to never speak of the Falls was a rule they both gladly abided by.

But one couldn't be too careful these days. Especially with Richard on the scene. The situation required constant vigilance.

Marvis and Roland stood at the outer edge of dancers, both of them looking at their feet. It appeared that Marvis was doing more talking than dancing. Roland glanced up and caught Delphine's gaze. He wore an expression that made him look like a gazelle who had recently been asked out to coffee by a hungry cheetah.

Delphine smiled and resumed watching the room. She decided to go and see what Richard, Ship, and Franko were up to.

The music started up as she crossed the studio, and she heard Roland call her name. His voice sounded desperate, but she continued her trek toward the group of men. If Roland could handle the streets of south Florida, he could handle a dance lesson from Marvis.

"Delphine!" said Franko, holding his arms wide as she approached.

"Franko," she answered, and let herself be swallowed by his friendly embrace.

Richard offered no greeting, instead taking a sip of whatever was in his paper cup.

"Hey babe," said Ship, and reached both arms out to her in expectation of a hug.

"Come any closer and I'll pop you in the acorns," she said.

Ship opened his arms wider and aimed his palms at the ceiling in a gesture of resignation. He turned to Richard. "On the dance floor, she can't get enough of me. Off the dance floor, she's as cold as a fish on antidepressants."

Richard shook his head as if to indicate her refusal to play nice was a real shame.

"Women, am I right?" said Delphine, and clenched her right fist, in case she felt like using it in the next ten seconds.

"Look at this crowd. Isn't it great?" Franko pointed to the dance floor. "I was just telling Mr. Dere here that our attendance has been trending upward over the last few months."

"Still thinking of buying the place?" she asked Richard.

"You wanna buy a dance studio?" Shipley asked Richard. "You never told me that!"

"It's not like we're beasties," snapped Richard.

"I think you mean—"

But Delphine didn't bother letting Ship finish correcting their former boss. "Richard, where's your wife this evening?"

"She's home with a headache tonight. She wanted to come though. She's really taking to water the fish. I mean like a fish to dancing. Well, she's getting the hang of it, anyway."

"I'm sure she is," said Delphine. "I guess you should probably buy the studio for her."

"Well now," said Franko, "we haven't talked specifics yet. I'm not even sure I want to sell."

"You'd probably change your mind if I made you an offer you

couldn't refuse," said Richard, breaking into his best Vito Corleone voice. Delphine clenched her fist again as the men guffawed.

Then they all fell silent and watched the dancing, which was in full swing now. Ella Fitzgerald's "Cheek to Cheek" kept time for everyone on the dance floor. Except for Roland, who was clearly having trouble finding his rhythm—if he had any to begin with.

Delphine decided to go for it. "Remember Simon? He was such a good dancer, wasn't he?"

"Simon! Geez, I haven't thought of him in years," said Ship.

"Simon Pegbottam?" asked Richard.

"Such a nice man," said Delphine. "Left behind a wife and daughter, if I recall correctly."

"Who's Pigbottom?" asked Franko.

"Simon Pegbottam was a colleague of ours, many years ago. Wonderful dancer," Delphine said to Franko.

"He was pretty good," said Ship. "But he had a lot more experience than we did. He was older. You and I are much better than he ever was, babe."

"He also knew a lot about cheese," she said.

Richard took another sip from his cup but this time seemed to choke on the liquid. He began coughing violently.

"Oh boy, Mitzi's coming this way, I gotta run," said Ship.

Delphine wondered if his sudden departure was because he was trying to avoid Mitzi or because he wanted to try and catch her. In any case, he was gone in a flash and try as she could, she couldn't find Mitzi in the crowd anywhere. Or Ship, for that matter.

Richard kept coughing. "You should get that looked at," said Delphine.

Richard caught his breath. "It's nobody. I mean not a problem."

Delphine had wanted to gauge his reaction when she brought up her old friend's name, and he hadn't disappointed. She wondered even more now if he'd had something to do with Simon's death.

"You should invite Pigbottom to come along sometime," suggested Franko.

"Well I would," she said, "but he's dead."

"Probably not a great dancer anymore then," said Franko. "And why aren't *you* out there tonight?"

"Because you haven't asked me yet," she said.

"Then let's go, m'dear!" Franko reached for her hand, and they walked onto the dance floor.

# CHAPTER 11

A Glenn Miller song came over the speakers, and Delphine and Franko started to dance. American foxtrot was just one of her specialties; Ship's too. They usually stuck with what they knew best, and that was how they'd won so many competitions.

Franko was also a pro. She hadn't danced as often with him though, so she wasn't as used to how he moved. They kept to a closed foxtrot step until they got their bearings, then performed a twinkle and switched to a promenade, which was an open step that allowed them to move around the floor.

"Take me closer to Ship," Delphine said. The two of them glided along and Delphine kept a sharp eye on her target, who was promenading with Mitzi on the far side of the crowd. At one point Ship performed an underarm turn with his partner, who laughed with delight as her sparkly earrings flashed.

"Jealous most?" asked Franko, who winked at her.

"I believe the phrase is jealous *much*," said Delphine, "and no, not in the least. But I do need to keep an eye on Shipley."

"Why didn't you say so?" said Franko. "Let's go!"

Delphine wanted to point out that she *had* said so, but let it go as Franko began to lengthen their strides to move them across the dance floor in half the time it would normally take. Then he took up a position trailing Ship and Mitzi, so that Delphine was nearest to Ship. Franko again switched his pace, and they settled into a leisurely rhythm to match the other two dancers.

Delphine smiled at Franko and mouthed the words, *thank you.* Franko winked at her again.

It was more difficult that she thought it would be to keep within hearing range of Ship. She wasn't sure it would matter, since he probably wouldn't reveal anything of interest to Mitzi. And they didn't seem to be saying all that much, except Delphine did hear the words *partner* and *competition* a few times.

Delphine still wanted to win the upcoming dance competition, but these days, the price might just be too high. Ship had only recently started calling her babe, and it was not a pleasant development. Maybe the man was getting cocky. They won every competition together, after all. Perhaps it was time for her to consider a partner change. But to whom? Franko was good, but Marvis would never let him dance with anyone else, and Delphine understood that. Well, that question would have to wait until all this cheese nonsense was over with.

Thanks to Franko's expert guidance, they danced up alongside Ship and Mitzi for a few moments more and this time, Delphine heard the words *my place* and … Had he just said the word *car*?

"Closer!" she whispered to Franko.

"If I get much closer, you're going to trip on Mitzi," said Franko, sounding a little annoyed.

Dancing with a partner was a lot like working with a partner on a mission for the Falls. Each person relied on the other for their own safety, and in turn always had the other person's back. And when two dancers were in sync and in the flow, the overall effect, the whole result, was always greater than the sum of its parts. Two partners working together always accomplished more than two people working by themselves.

But when two people weren't in sync, the sum might equal a lot less than the individual parts. In Delphine's haste to stay near Ship, she pulled on Franko, who hadn't been expecting it, and they lost their synchronization, spinning off their intended path like a Formula One car missing a hairpin curve. They moved to the edge of the crowd and stopped dancing.

"Your mind's not on your feet," said Franko, a little out of breath from the surprise moves.

He was right, of course, and Delphine felt bad. Her mind had been on bigger things—rightfully so, but that didn't mean it was okay to put Franko in danger of injury. "I'm sorry," she said. "You're right."

He looked at her a little more closely. "Is everything okay?"

"Oh yes," she said, and faked a laugh. "Everything is fine. Let's take a little break."

They stood together and watched the dancing for a few moments. She spotted Roland and Marvis. Roland was still looking at his feet most of the time, and his tongue stuck out one corner of his mouth in concentration, like a little kid. Delphine smiled at that, and then had to laugh as she watched Marvis pull her hand away from his hip and tilt his chin up so their eyes met.

Delphine noticed Franko was watching his wife too. "Jealous most?" she asked him.

"She'd never go for him. He might be handsome as all get-out, but look at him! He's a terrible dancer," said Franko.

Delphine smiled. "He sure is."

They chatted for a moment about nothing in particular, until suddenly their attention, along with everyone else's on the dance floor, was drawn to a spot a few yards away, where a male figure lay prone on the floor, one knee pulled up to his chest while his hands clutched at his calf. Roland.

"Man down, man down!" said Ship, who ran to Roland and knelt beside him.

By his time everyone had stopped dancing and Delphine grimaced at the sight of her partner rolling on the floor, debilitated by a charley horse.

"Franko, can you help me with something? Send Ship away from there, would you?" Delphine whispered in her friend's ear.

"You bet." Franko stood tall and waded into the crowd toward Roland. "Make way, medical personnel!" It wasn't a lie, since Franko had been a surgeon before he retired and opened a dance studio.

Delphine slipped away and located Richard, who was now standing by the snack table holding a handful of Double Stuffy-O cookies.

"What's all the commotion?" he asked Delphine.

"Oh, it's nothing. Someone got a leg cramp." She motioned with her hand that it was no big deal, and with the other hand reached for a cookie. Ordinarily she would never eat something with palm oil, high fructose corn syrup, and the dreaded "natural flavors" mystery ingredient, but desperate times and all that.

Richard laughed. "With so many old geezers in this place, that's not very surprising."

She didn't have the heart to tell him the "geezer" in question was under the age of forty. It was always the noobs, no matter their age, who underestimated the level of physical strength, flexibility, and endurance ballroom dancing required. It was not a sport for the weak, and that was another reason she loved it, of course. She took a bite of cookie and winced at the cloying sweetness. Tasted like capitalism. She laughed at herself.

"Have you found out anything about those wheels of Beaufort d'Alpage?" she asked Richard.

"Still waiting for the fingerprint results."

Delphine imagined that in reality he was still figuring out how to doctor either the cheese or the paperwork to make it appear like she'd had her hands all over them. She hated to think that her boss had anything to do with setting her up, but how could she believe otherwise? But as of yet, she had no proof.

"Listen, Delphine," he said, leaning over to speak in a quieter voice. "We've known each other a long time. I sure would be disappointed to find out that you're not who you think I was—I mean, that I'm not who you used to be..." He stopped talking and huffed out a breath. "It'd be a shame to find out you've been up to something after all these years."

She would have said, "Likewise," but couldn't be sure of what she'd be agreeing with. Instead, she said, "Why do you suppose they've reemerged now? And why target me?"

Richard laughed. "You're suggesting it's someone else, but I need to follow the evidence, and right now the evidence points to you. So perhaps the question should be, why did you slip up and get caught? Maybe you're tossing your lunch. I mean, losing your touchings."

Delphine had nothing to say to that. The man had an annoying habit of confusing his words, but there was no confusing his intention. He was smart. But she was smarter, and she knew she would prevail. If something bad didn't happen to her first.

"Here comes Ship," said Richard. "Maybe he can fill us in on the injured guy."

"Excuse me," she said, and slipped away from the table just as Ship walked up. She went down the hall toward the bathroom, waited ten seconds, and came back out again, tossing the rest of her Stuffy-O in a nearby trash can. Careful to stay out of Richard and Ship's sight as she inched her way back to them, she used other people for cover, and managed to get within hearing distance.

"What did you find out?" Ship asked.

"Nothing useful," said Richard.

"Well, try harder," said Ship in a sharp tone.

"Watch it, Ship. I'm still your boss."

Ship laughed nervously. "Right, right. Do you have my money?"

Richard said, "Not yet, but I have to go—"

And then Delphine was jostled by Roland, who clung to Marvis' arm with one hand and reached out to her with the other.

"I'm dying!" he yelled.

# CHAPTER 12

Delphine sat at the center island, sipping tea, as Roland drank a glass of water and paced the kitchen with a prominent limp. Kenji had come over shortly after the Mercedes had pulled into the garage, and now stood by the island sink fixing himself a peanut butter sandwich.

"The evening was a bit of a bust," admitted Delphine.

"I don't know," said Roland. "I think maybe I got the hang of the foxtrot." He winced and reached down to massage his left calf. "Sort of."

"You are not in very good shape," said Kenji.

"I'm in fine shape. It's just been a long day, and I was dehydrated. Could've happened to anyone." He felt his face turn red at the thought of the scene he'd made, rolling around on the floor of a dance studio with thirty-plus seniors watching. He couldn't even keep up with a bunch of oldsters! That realization hit him like a baseball bat. Within the space of a day, he'd gone from Florida detective to Pasadena ballroom dancer. What was next, knitting?

"The sport is more demanding than most people realize," said Kenji in a tone that Roland assumed was supposed to approximate sympathy.

"Oh my god," said Roland. "Please stop."

"You told me you were dying," said Delphine with a grin.

"It felt like I was! That was the most painful leg cramp I've ever had."

"Real men dance," Kenji went on.

"Do you go?" Roland asked him.

"Heck no."

"Don't you ever go dancing with your wife?" Delphine asked him.

"She likes to read," Roland said, and hoped Delphine would drop the subject. Dancing had been a sore spot in the early days of his marriage; Christina always wanted to go to salsa clubs, but he'd refused, and she moped about it. Eventually she stopped asking, and now she went dancing a few times a month with a friend. At least that was where she always said she was going.

Kenji shook his head in disappointment. "You do not communicate with her," he told Roland.

"Did they train you for psychological warfare?" Roland asked him. "Because you are brutal."

Kenji shrugged.

"Roland, did you see or hear anything unusual out on the dance floor?" Delphine asked, mercifully changing the subject.

"No, sorry. I spent most of my energy trying to pay attention to Marvis." Roland put down his water glass and held out his arms in front of him. "Slow, slow, quick-quick. Slow, slow, qui—ow!"

As Roland attempted to glide around the kitchen without hitting anything or doubling over in pain, Delphine told them about her conversation with Richard and Ship, and what she overheard them say at the snack table.

"So Richard did not incriminate himself," said Kenji.

"Correct," said Delphine. "And still seems to think it was my cheese. Roland, could you slow down, dear? You're making me nervous."

Roland came to a stop next to her and took another drink of his water.

Delphine said, "It sounded to me like something was going on between Richard and Shipley, but it was impossible to tell if one of them might be … in charge."

"You mean you couldn't tell if one of them was the Big Cheese?" asked Roland, and she nodded.

"It could be either of them, or it could be neither of them," said Kenji.

"You are a sage," said Delphine. Then she frowned. "I just can't help feeling that Richard is up to something."

"Do we have access to the old case files?" asked Roland.

"No," she said. "And even if we did, it would be impossible to tell if the information was accurate. Who knows what they're up to? I'll bet you dollars to Danish fontina that they're going to tell me my fingerprints are on those wheels of cheese."

"I would not be surprised," agreed Kenji.

"But no word on that yet?" asked Roland.

"Still waiting," she said.

The room was silent for a few beats while they thought about the situation.

"Let's see. Someone out there is putting your fingerprints on some cheese. Your old boss seems interested in buying a dance studio, and is implying you had something to do with the death of your colleague forty years ago," said Roland.

"That's about right," she said.

Kenji put more peanut butter on his slice of bread. "I wonder if Walter Shipley is le Grande Fromage."

"His French always was rather good," said Delphine.

"All conjecture," said Roland, as he began to pace around the kitchen island again. "There's too much I don't know. *We* don't know. How does any of this connect to your past case, and how does your past case connect to right now? I have no idea what anything means." He looked at Delphine. "Do you?"

Delphine tilted her head in thought.

"And why the heck are we supposed to go to an underground cheese hideout?"

"It's the Underground Cheese Consortium," said Delphine.

"It could be an underwater cheese amusement park for all I care," said Roland. Frustration began to well in his chest. He'd tried to take the day in stride, but he was tired, didn't understand how any of the scant information he'd received fit together, and now he was also hungry for a sandwich. He stopped pacing and stood next to Kenji, who had already placed a slice of bread on the cutting board for him, as if reading his mind. Again. He handed the knife to Roland.

"What I want to know is, if this whooooole thing is a big fuss about some dumb fancy cheese, how come we're sitting here eating this stuff?" Roland held up the knife with a huge dollop of peanut butter balanced on the edge, then spread it all over the bread. "Where's the cheese?"

"I don't eat much cheese these days," said Delphine.

"That's ironic," said Roland.

"I don't eat it often either," said Kenji. "It makes me burp."

"You two are a regular barrel of fun," muttered Roland.

Kenji brightened at that. "I am very regular!" he said.

"Delphine, please make him stop," said Roland.

Delphine went to Kenji and put her hand on his shoulder. "Kenji, we'd better get to bed. Maybe you should go on home."

"That sounds reasonable," said Kenji. "I will take the rest of my sandwich to go." He walked to the sliding door that led to the patio.

Roland assumed the man came and went as he pleased via the backyard. Like they were kids—best friends living across the street from each other, climbing in through the window when their parents were asleep.

Kenji put his hand on the sliding door handle and when he'd pulled it open about a foot, they heard a strange sound coming from the side of the house. *Scrape. Thump. Scrape. Thump.*

They all froze, and Roland looked at Delphine, whose eyes

were as wide as the tires on her E-class. Kenji moved away from the door and back into the kitchen.

*Scrape. Thump.*

"It's…" said Delphine.

"It is what?" asked Kenji.

"Richard," she whispered. "That's his uneven gait. He's in the backyard!"

Roland raced to the guest room, retrieved his weapon, and ran back to the kitchen. Kenji had moved to the wall, trying to listen to the sound. Delphine still stood frozen at the kitchen island.

"He is at the corner of the house," said Kenji, motioning to the sliding door.

"Let me go check," said Delphine.

"Don't be ridiculous," said Roland, and when her face morphed into a scowl, he immediately regretted his words. Steam had started to form behind her eyes and was in danger of coming out her ears.

"I mean I'm here, so let me look into it," he said in a voice he hoped sounded contrite.

"No time to discuss semantics," whispered Kenji. "Roland. Go."

Roland nodded and crept to the door, gun drawn. His stress level was high, but so was his excitement. When Delphine had first told him why he was there, and that it was all about some smelly French cheese, he'd been more than a little disappointed. Cheese! It was laughable. And then the ballroom dancing had almost been too much. But now things were getting interesting. This was good.

The lights in the backyard were off, and Roland moved to the switch, to the right of the back door. Kenji nodded again, indicating that Richard was still at the corner of the house. Which was strange—if he was walking, how come his position hadn't changed? But Roland didn't think too hard about it. The first order of business was neutralizing the threat.

In one quick, seamless motion, Roland switched on the light, squeezed through the opening in the sliding door, and headed to the side of the house. And stopped.

"Where is he?" asked Delphine as she and Kenji rushed to his side. "Oh."

They watched as a squirrel tried to bury something under the canopy of a ficus tree planted in a big clay pot. Every time the squirrel dug, it made the ficus tree move and the branches scraped the wooden columns of the pergola. *Scrape. Thump.*

"Unless that squirrel's name is Richard, I think we've got the wrong man," said Roland, lowering his weapon.

"Nuts," said Kenji.

"I … I'm so sorry," said Delphine, who looked downright puzzled. "It sounded just like Richard's footsteps."

"I think we're all a little jittery," said Roland. "We all need some sleep."

"Yes," said Delphine.

"Get good rest tonight," said Kenji, putting a hand on Delphine's shoulder. "Tomorrow you go to the UCC. See where the path leads you. Maybe you will get a sign from the universe!"

Roland laughed but realized no one else was joining in. "What, you weren't kidding?"

"Don't you get hunches?" Delphine asked him.

"Sure, but those are just, you know, ideas."

"Yes, but you never know when or from where those ideas come from, do you?" said Kenji.

Roland thought about it and realized he didn't have an answer. But still. The *universe?* Please. "Nope, that's dumb."

Kenji gave Delphine another one of his looks that seemed to indicate he felt bad for her having to deal with such an unenlightened partner. Or maybe Kenji felt sorry for him; it was hard to say. In any case, it was annoying.

"Let's go to bed," said Delphine.

They watched as Kenji disappeared around the side of the

house. Roland didn't want to say anything, but he felt very disappointed that he hadn't gotten to catch anything more suspicious than a squirrel. Suddenly, all the adrenaline from the day's events wore off at once and he felt tired and alone. Cheese, squirrels, dancing … He just wanted to go home.

# CHAPTER 13

"Welcome to downtown LA," Delphine said, pointing out the window at the fast-approaching (as fast as traffic would allow, which wasn't very fast) cluster of skyscrapers.

"Thrilled to be here," said Roland with a hefty dose of sarcasm.

Delphine clenched her jaw. Under normal circumstances she wouldn't tolerate such insolence from a subordinate, but she would give him a little more time to adjust. She had, after all, plucked him from his life in Florida and brought him into a strange and stressful situation.

It was right after 11:00 a.m. by the time they arrived downtown. They'd gotten up early to attend a yoga class at Delphine's favorite studio. Roland had never done yoga before, and put up a mighty stink about going, but she reminded him that she could have a very large impact on his life with one very short phone call, and he acquiesced. Once he realized he wasn't the only man in the class, he loosened up a bit. He didn't say much afterward, but she could tell he'd enjoyed it. Never mind the fact he'd looked as awkward as a giraffe on roller skates.

"Is your leg feeling better?" she asked.

"I think so, yeah," he said. "I'm telling you, I'm in great shape."

"Right."

She still felt bad about the night before, mistaking a squirrel in one of her potted plants for Richard's awkward gait right outside her back door. She'd thought about it as she fell asleep—how could she have thought a rodent sounded like Richard? Well, actually that was kind of funny, since she sometimes thought of Richard as a rat. But still. It had been embarrassing. She wanted to apologize to Roland again, but knew that when playing a man's game, apologies were suicide. So she skipped it and remained silent.

They exited the freeway and crawled through the downtown streets. Smaller buildings were nestled throughout the towering structures, but it still felt like one solid mass to Delphine, and she marveled at the city's denseness every time she visited. Which wasn't very often these days.

She drove Roland past City Hall, hoping his sense of duty as a police detective would help him rise to the occasion. "We're going to have lunch while we're here. How's your French?"

"Excuse me?" Roland said.

"Do you like cheese?"

Delphine pulled into an almost-empty parking lot after flashing something at the attendant and parked her Mercedes. When she turned off the engine and looked at Roland, he was staring at her with a blank expression.

"Tu parles français, non?" she asked. "Aimes tu le fromage?"

Nothing.

Delphine looked back at the dashboard and thought for a moment. She considered waiting in the car while she sent him inside, to avoid the possibility of being recognized by anyone. But that would probably be too much for the poor fellow. They needed to go in together. She just hoped she wouldn't regret her decision.

"Let's go," she said.

Roland swung his gaze from the parking attendant, who stood in the center of the lot dancing to music only she could hear, back to Delphine. "Go where?"

"There." She pointed to a stately building from a past era. Half of it was six stories tall, the other half only three.

"Not exactly a skyscraper," said Roland.

"The Grand Central Market opened in 1917. Los Angeles had a law restricting all buildings to less than thirteen stories until 1958."

"You're sh—I mean, kidding me."

"No, I am not." Delphine opened her door and gathered her purse. "Let's go in."

"Have you ever thought about retiring?" he asked as he got out of the car and shut the passenger door.

"This is as close to retirement as I can get. In case you haven't noticed, in my line of work you're never entirely out of the business."

"All I know is, when I leave the force, I'm leaving for good," he said.

Delphine knew better but kept it to herself. Maybe he would be one of the lucky ones to disengage from his former, all-consuming life … Time would tell.

They walked into the building and were engulfed in a crowd of tourists and locals milling around the large open space of the first floor. Fresh produce spilled from wooden crates, people behind counters shouted orders to chefs. There was food everywhere, in all forms. Prepared, fresh, cooked, raw. Delphine smiled. She loved this place—the noise and the culinary assault on the senses. She looked at Roland, who was wide-eyed but didn't seem to be overwhelmed.

"Why did we come at such a busy time?" he asked.

"The UCC is only open from ten to three. Besides, the crowds help us blend in." She wove around and through the crowds at a speed that Roland seemed to have difficulty keeping up with. At one point she narrowly avoided colliding with a large man dressed in all white save for a stained, greasy apron.

"Lady, you don't blend in anywhere," said Roland.

Delphine pulled out the note Kenji had given her. She guided them through crowd to a quiet corner, where she opened an unmarked door and led them down a long hallway.

"Do you have your weapon?" she asked Roland as she reached in her purse and ran her fingers along the handle of her .38.

"No," he said.

"What? Why not?"

"It's at your house." He stopped walking. "It's not like I have a lot of places on me to conceal it. And it's way too hot for a jacket." He turned his palms upward and gestured at his muscular torso.

Delphine took note of his attire: a light-grey T-shirt, jeans, and Doc Martens. A gun would have stood out like an extra bulging pec muscle. "Come on then," she said.

They stopped at another unmarked door and Delphine reached for the handle, but it opened before she had a chance to grip it. Out came a slim young woman wearing black capris and a crisp white shirt, and a man with long sideburns dressed in a turtleneck like Steve McQueen in *Bullitt*. The pair gave Delphine and Roland looks of curiosity. Delphine paid them no attention.

"You could pull off dressing like that," she said to Roland once they were down the next hallway a few yards, eyeing his T-shirt.

Roland laughed. "Every cop dreams of looking as cool as McQueen."

Delphine didn't doubt it.

They went down three flights of stairs and a minute later stood in front of a pair of grey metal double doors guarded by a long-haired man in white painter's overalls, lounging in a folding chair. An open five-gallon container of paint sat next to him on the floor, with a handle sticking out that presumably belonged to a paint roller.

"Kraft Parmesan," Delphine said.

The man nodded once, stood up, and opened the door closest to him. As they passed by, Delphine stole a glance into the bucket. It was a third full of dried paint, the roller forever cemented in its chemical grave. A few cigarette butts littered the top of the dried paint. It was obvious that this place was secret, but the atmosphere was so casual that it must have been an open secret.

The man closed the door behind them, and that was when the smell infiltrated her nostrils. Sharp cheeses, hard cheeses, soft ones and moldy ones. Delphine inhaled deeply right as Roland's stomach growled.

The space was enormous, but not packed with people. Industrial-strength fluorescent lights illuminated the room, but every other bulb was either broken or shut off on purpose, creating a dim environment. Maybe twenty-five booths of various sizes were set up to create a big square, and a smaller square of more booths were set up inside the larger one. A few food vendors with makeshift kitchens lined the walls, each with its own small grouping of tables and chairs.

"Why such a big deal about cheese?" asked Roland. "I mean, it's just … cheese!"

"There are hundreds, if not thousands of types of cheese," said Delphine. "What we see in our local grocery store chains is such a small representation of what's being produced. This place offers true connoisseurs a chance to buy and sell rare and expensive cheeses."

"Are all of these illegal?"

"No, but a lot of them probably are."

They walked a few steps farther into the large room. She watched Roland's face as he took everything in for the first time. She hadn't been to the UCC before either, but thanks to Operation Big Cheese, she was more familiar with the shadow world of cheese than he was. Therefore, she could anticipate his next question.

"We had to investigate French cheese specifically because production in France is much stricter. The government gives a special designation to certain regional cheeses if they're made following a strict set of specifications, and products that carry that designation are worth a lot more. To bring in those cheeses without paying tariffs could prove very detrimental to the overall economy."

Roland gave her a skeptical look now. "Come on," he said. "It's not like we're talking barrels of oil from the Mideast or something."

"No, but many French people take cheese just as seriously as many Saudis take their crude oil."

"Huh," was all he said.

Explaining everything to Roland seemed to open the floodgates on her memories of the past Big Cheese case, and her life at that time. Her dear husband Charles had still been alive. She'd become a mother. She was young, healthy, and nothing stood in her way. Nostalgia and sadness overcame her almost as strongly as the scents of exotic cheeses.

"What now?" said Roland, his hands stuffed in his pockets.

"I'm going to hang back. You start in the center and then work your way down the tables along the wall. We'll meet over there at that sign that says, 'Cheese Lounge.'" She pointed to the back of the room at a green sign with yellow lettering attached to a stanchion post. "Go talk to people, see what they're selling. Keep a sharp eye out for French cheeses."

"Was that a joke?" he asked.

Delphine made a face. Funny guy.

Roland frowned. "I don't know anything about cheese except that cheddar is the orange one."

"You can tell by the names what country they're from, and by talking to people. But don't sound too innocent, or you'll tip them off. What am I saying? You know how to do stuff like this. Now get going."

"Okay, boss."

Roland wandered off and Delphine pulled her reading glasses out of her purse so she could inspect the goods up close. She stayed along the perimeter of the room, keeping her head down and only making eye contact with people when necessary. When she did interact with vendors, she kept a neutral expression on her face. Samples were being handed out at many tables, and she picked up a bit of incredible gorgonzola and a tasty Maasdam.

With a moment to reflect on the last few days, she had to admit she felt bad about blindsiding Roland. She knew what it was like to be expected to show up for a job without being told much of anything, which gave her empathy for the man. After spending more time with him that morning, her gut instinct confirmed she could trust him, and that somehow—she didn't know the particulars, but somehow—he would prove critical to getting past this mess. She knew she'd made the right call.

Once she made a cursory check of the restaurant vendors, she headed toward the sign for the Cheese Lounge. Behind the row of stanchions was another set of metal double doors, and as she got closer, she could hear the faint sound of music—Sinatra, if she wasn't mistaken, and she knew she wasn't. The smell of exotic cheeses, mixed with something a little more herbal, wafted by. What a fascinating place this was! Now that she knew it was here, she'd have to come back sometime to partake. In the cheese.

She surveyed the entirety of the room while she waited for Roland. Any one of the people in this room or in the Lounge could be the Big Cheese. It felt like trying to find a cheese curd in a dairy farm.

Before she could become too despondent about their chances of making any progress, Roland walked up with a wad of napkins in one hand, and a half-eaten grilled-cheese sandwich in the other.

"Best damn sandwich I've ever had. Hands down." He took another bite. "Some kind of gruyere with caramelized onions. Mmm! Fu—"

"Just stop," interrupted Delphine. It did smell delicious, but she'd lost her appetite once they'd entered the building. "Did you see anything?"

Roland swallowed and wiped his fingers on a napkin. "Not really," he said. "But someone saw you."

"What?"

"There's a woman back there who says she knows you. Come with me."

The two of them walked away from the Cheese Lounge, and Delphine let Roland lead her down the side of the building. Her tension level began to increase the farther they went. They veered off the main path created by the outer row of booths and headed for a display that was set up all on its own, right alongside the wall. Three six-foot folding tables were set up in a "U" shape, allowing buyers to peruse the outer side of the U. A tent covered the space, even though they were indoors, and a woman wearing a sweatshirt that said *BITCHIN'* on the front sat behind the tables.

"Hello, Delphine," the woman said as Roland brought them to a stop.

Delphine gave the woman a terse smile. "Hello, Sylvie."

# CHAPTER 14

They joined Sylvie behind her cheese display and Roland pulled out a chair so Delphine could sit next to her friend. Or was she a nemesis? Time would tell. He took care to sit a little apart from the two women so he could observe them better.

But as soon as he sat, his mind wandered, as it had multiple times since he'd first seen Delphine standing there in the airport. He tried to dismiss the fact that he'd essentially been bushwhacked, or whatever the bureaucratic word for "abducting for business purposes" was. His anger kept bubbling up, even though he tried not to let it bother him. If he thought about it, so far the assignment hadn't been too taxing. Some cheese, a charley horse, and some decent food. He even thought the yoga had been okay.

Delphine caught his eye and gave him a look of admonishment, like a disapproving schoolteacher catching her pupil daydreaming. He shrugged and reached for a paper plate loaded with cheese samples. He loved cheese, but he was unsure whether cheese loved him back. He might have fibbed a bit when he'd said he wasn't lactose intolerant.

"I'm surprised to see you here," Delphine said.

"What else would I be doing?" asked the woman in a thick

French accent. "After what happened, I didn't have many choices other than underground cheese monger."

"I think it was a little more complicated than that," said Delphine. "What happened to you? One day you just vanished, and the operation closed down."

Sylvie inspected the top of her right hand and shrugged. "Ask Richard."

Delphine lowered her head. "About that…"

Sylvie was silent, waiting for Delphine to finish, and Roland sat transfixed, watching them while munching on cheese samples. Each woman behaved like a cat—friendly enough, but their metaphorical ears and tails flicked as they sized each other up. It was like they were getting ready to pounce on each other. He'd never seen anything like it, and that was saying a lot.

The long silence continued, and Roland could tell Delphine was figuring out how to play the situation. He couldn't help her though, since he still wasn't exactly sure what was going on or who this person was. Even so, he could tell Delphine wanted to know something, and Sylvie had no intention of telling her anything.

"I never thought you were le Grande Fromage," Delphine finally said.

Roland got out his phone to translate the foreign-sounding words into English. *The Big Cheese.* Oh, right.

Sylvie scoffed. "And why would you?"

"Because we were told it was you," said Delphine. "And that you'd escaped. But I never did buy it."

"Yes, well," said Sylvie. "I made a few mistakes. I was less experienced then." She turned to Roland and gave him a head-to-toe once-over before looking him in the eye and raising one eyebrow. "We do impulsive things when we are young. But as we grow older, we develop better control of desires."

Roland felt a little warm under his nonexistent collar. She was a beautiful woman, but probably only slightly younger than

Delphine. Still, it was uncomfortable to be stared at like a … piece of cheese.

"I'm sorry if you got caught up in something untoward all those years ago," said Delphine. "But please, now you have a chance to help me."

"I do?" Sylvie sounded offended. "That is rich! I haven't heard from you in years, and here you are asking for help. For what? I don't know."

Delphine looked worried, but her voice contained no emotion when she spoke. "If you know of anything going on now that is connected to that case, you've got to tell me."

"I don't have to tell you anything!" said Sylvie. "Oh, let me guess, I should do it because we women should stick together. Because we need to have each other's backs in this age of empowerment. Well, ma soeur, I watch no one's back but my own." She crossed her arms and glowered at Delphine.

Roland began to worry the two women might come to blows. Whatever Delphine wanted from Sylvie, it was clear she wasn't going to get it anytime soon. He picked up the last piece of cheese on his plate. "This is good. What is it?" He popped the morsel in his mouth without waiting for an answer.

Delphine remained quiet while Sylvie's gaze wandered to Roland again. Her glare was replaced by a devious smile, and her eyes slid to his left arm. Then something in the distance, over his shoulder, caught her attention. Her eyes narrowed for a moment before she regained her composure.

"I'm just asking for a lead," said Delphine.

*Wrong move*, thought Roland. Too direct. It was time to turn up the charm. Perhaps he could help after all.

"And what's in it for me?" Sylvie asked, looking at Roland's left thigh now.

Delphine threw up her hands in frustration.

He set the empty paper plate on the nearest table, crossed his legs, and leaned one elbow on the top of his thigh. Then he pointed to one of the small restaurants and said, "Delphine, would you go over there, and get me another one of those grilled cheese with onion sandwiches?" He flashed her a bland smile, hoping she'd catch on. She did.

She stood up and pulled her purse tightly to her side. "I'm sorry, Sylvie. I really am." And then she left.

Roland slid his folding chair closer to Sylvie. "I'm still hungry," he said, backing up his innuendo with a look that was as close to lascivious as he could get under the circumstances.

"Yes, well, we do have many fine things to choose from here," she said in a pleasant tone.

He flexed his left quad muscles a few times. "I can tell that you still hold a grudge against Delphine," he began. "I would too. Maybe you think she threw you under the bus somehow. But personally, I don't think she did. And maybe this is an opportunity for the truth to finally come to light. You have a chance to help someone here. Isn't there anything you can tell me?"

She still looked skeptical. Time to break out the big guns. He glanced down at his right arm, drawing her eyes there too, and flexed his bicep. Of all the reasons to work out, he'd never realized that seducing a senior-citizen informant would be one of the benefits.

Sylvie looked at his bare arm. Her mouth was closed, but one end quirked up. "You're good, sonny, but not that good."

"You have no idea," he said, cool as a cucumber.

She laughed. "Okay, fine. Look, all I know is that someone that we knew back then called me out of the blue three weeks ago. I had not heard from him in years, and suddenly he's asking me for four wheels of a very—and I mean very—expensive cheese."

"Name?"

"Beaufort d'Alpage."

"Beauford who?"

Sylvie gave him a blank look. "The cheese. It was a Beaufort. If you are looking for the name of the individual, that will cost you."

"Cost me what, exactly?"

"I will think about that one."

Roland ran his fingers through his hair. "There has to be something you can tell me about this person other than it was someone from your past."

"Oui. This individual came to me a few weeks ago, asking me to procure this rare cheese. He did not tell me why he needed it, nor did I ask. But now perhaps I'm regretting my involvement."

"Are you … the Big Cheese?" he asked her. He felt funny using such a silly name for what everyone seemed to think was a serious situation.

Sylvie's laugh sounded like silver. "Non, Monsieur Roland. Non."

"Then how did you get this fancy cheese if you're not in the game?"

"Oh, that's an easy one. I have many friends here," she said, and gestured at the room. "There are a few people here who owe me favors, and I can procure almost any cheese I want."

Roland was familiar with how that worked—it was the same whether you were dealing in cheese or stolen bowling balls or anything else, for that matter. Favors were often called in for better or worse. "Maybe one of those people is the head cheese," he suggested.

Sylvie gave him a sour face. "Head cheese? I think you are confusing your foods." She eyed his thigh again. "Anyway, as far as I know, Mister Policeman, there is no Big Cheese anymore. If there is one, they are very good at keeping quiet. Or maybe someone is about to start up the operation again. Like your friend Delphine, perhaps?"

Roland shook his head. "Nope, not her."

"How can you be sure? You haven't known her very long."

While that was true, Roland still didn't buy the attempt at misdirection. "I follow my gut, and my gut says she's not in the cheese business."

"Would your gut like another sample?" asked Sylvie. She reached for a small cube of cheese with tiny little holes in it, slid her chair closer to his, and popped the delectable bite of dairy into his mouth.

"What is that?" he asked in a dreamy voice.

"That is the Chevrotin, from Haute-Savoie region. Pretty good, non?"

"Weeeeee," said Roland, trying to recall how to pronounce the basics that he'd learned from his one year of French in high school. "One more thing though. Who did you get the Beaufort from? It's okay, you can tell me." He flexed his bicep again.

Sylvie watched with amusement and then said, "This is the funny part. I could not get the Beaufort d'Alpage for my friend."

"Oh," said Roland. "Wait, what?" He stood up so quickly the chair skidded on the cement floor. "Why didn't you lead with that information?"

"You didn't ask," she said, taking his hand and pulling him to sit back down in the chair.

"Where did the cheese come from then?"

"I have no idea," said Sylvie. "Honestly. I am telling you everything now. Although why I am helping, I still don't know. Anyway, I could not find it. Four wheels of this cheese is worth a fortune, and no one had that much. I might have been looking around at starting up the operation again, so I had been looking for French connections. But I found nothing."

Roland tapped his chin. "I wonder where it came from."

"This is what I would like to know also." Sylvie looked over his shoulder again. "Now as much as I'd love to sample your merchandise like you've been sampling mine, I suggest you and Delphine leave right this minute, unless you want to meet with an unfortunate cheese slicer accident." She nodded to his left and he turned in time to see two very large, angry-looking men coming their way. Sylvie slipped a small paper bag into his hands and pushed him out from behind the cheese display.

# CHAPTER 15

Roland found Delphine at the grilled cheese vendor. "We've got company," he said, and then winced because he sounded like a goofy TV cop on the *Hawaii Five-0* remake rather than a special agent on an important cheese-related mission. His wife loved that damn show. He hated it, although the scenery looked awfully nice.

"What are you talking about?" asked Delphine.

He pointed to the two large men coming their way. The two thugs would be on them soon, cutting off the route to the doors Roland and Delphine had entered through.

Delphine took his arm. "Come on," she said, and pulled him toward the Cheese Lounge.

"What about my sandwich?" he asked.

Delphine didn't bother replying and continued to head for the lounge at a brisk pace.

"That's awfully risky," he said. "If there's no exit in there up to the main floor of the building…"

"We're toasted, yes," said Delphine. She opened one of the double doors to the Lounge and shoved Roland inside before entering herself.

"I think you mean toast?" Roland instinctively put an arm

around Delphine as they tried to get their bearings. "Oh, wait. I get it. Like grilled cheese."

"That's my boy," said Delphine. "Now get your hands off me."

"Sabotage" by the Beastie Boys blared on the sound system, and the lighting was so dim that Roland hoped his eyes adjusted before he ran into anything that might cause him trouble. From what he could see, the center of the room was full of pub tables, and more vendors lined the walls. Along one entire wall ran a bar with backlit shelves full of liquor bottles from counter to ceiling.

The space was maybe half as big as the main one, and it was even more packed with people. Groups huddled around the pub tables, and food wasn't the only aroma in the air. Roland didn't want to think about what kind of cheesy deals went down in darkness of the Cheese Lounge.

"This way." Delphine took off toward the far wall, and he followed.

Roland's police instincts kicked into high gear. He half-wished he had his firearm with him. But using it in this space would be the worst idea possible, so it was just as well he was unarmed.

They sped on, and heads turned as they passed. Was it because they were moving so fast, or because no one recognized them, making it painfully obvious they shouldn't be there? Or perhaps they were surprised at the sight of a tall man running through a Cheese Lounge with a diminutive, white-haired speed demon.

"Hey man," said a voice to his right, and a hand reached out to grab his shoulder. Delphine disappeared into the crowd in front of him.

"What!" barked Roland as he turned and then looked up into the face of a big, burly man in a tight-fitting black T-shirt who'd latched onto his arm. By Roland's estimation, this guy was even bigger than the two who were coming for him and Delphine. "I mean, yes?"

"You can't run in here, man."

Roland wrenched his arm free and said, "Okay," as he took off to catch up with Delphine. He found her not too far up ahead, weaving her way through crowds of cheese lovers of all ages, sizes, and colors. Score one for cheese diversity, he thought.

He looked back long enough to see the entrance door closing behind the two thugs. "They've made us," he said, slipping into *Hawaii Five-0* speak again.

"Then hurry up," said Delphine, and surged ahead of him again.

As he passed by the bar, Roland noted it could provide cover for them if needed. But then he spotted what Delphine had already seen—an emergency exit door, straight ahead.

Delphine was a fair distance ahead of him now, and that meant she would get out of the building and make it back to her car. Perhaps at his expense though.

He watched as his partner reached the emergency exit door and pushed through. No alarm went off—a big plus. He needed to do something to buy them some time. He needed a diversion.

That was when he remembered he was still holding the bag Sylvie had given him. He stuck his hand into the opening of the crumpled paper sack and a few oversize thumbtacks jabbed into his fingertips.

"Mother—!" he yelled, and then emptied the contents of the bag behind him as he went through the emergency exit.

At the top of three flights of stairs, Delphine was waiting for him, not even winded, naturally. He nodded at her, for speaking would give his poor aerobic health away. They walked as fast as they could down yet another hallway and when they opened that door, they found themselves back in the crowds of the Grand Central Market.

"Do I have time to stop for a kombucha?" asked Roland as they walked past a shop called the Booch Bar.

But Delphine never answered, just kept on walking. They made it to the car, got in, and pulled out into traffic. It was then that he noticed he had a few thumbtacks stuck in the thumb and middle finger of his right hand. The spikes were long and sharp, dangerous enough to stop even the biggest of cheese thugs.

"What are those?" Delphine asked, looking at his hand.

"A gift from Sylvie," said Roland.

"Looks like a gift from the universe to me," she said, smiling.

Roland tried hard not to roll his eyes. "More importantly, who were those guys?"

"I wonder the same thing. They could have been the same men I saw near my car right before we found the Beaufort in my trunk."

"Maybe Judy did set you up after all," said Roland.

"Maybe," said Delphine, sounding lost in thought.

"I know you don't want to think that, but it's a possibility."

"I know. In any case, someone knows we're looking around." Delphine merged onto the 110 and they headed home.

# CHAPTER 16

"When can we go to the beach?" asked Roland as he slurped the remains of a green smoothie drink.

"No time for the beach," said Delphine. It was a true enough statement, but she also didn't have much patience these days for cross-town traffic. Driving to the airport to pick Roland up had been bad enough, but navigating coastal traffic would be even worse. She'd seen wars, explosions, and had even spent three days in a Swiss prison, but now, LA traffic was the most unbearable form of punishment of all.

"If everything works out, I will take you before you leave," said Kenji, also slurping a green drink.

"You've got beaches in Florida," said Delphine, grumpy that Kenji would go against her.

"Nuh-uh," said Roland. "I keep telling you. It's totally different here!" He placed his empty cup in a recycling bin, looked up at the clear blue sky, and took a deep breath. "This place has got a good vibe. Buena onda." The last two words were uttered in perfect Spanish and Delphine gasped. "What?" he asked.

"I had assumed you were bad with all languages, but I suppose it's just French."

"I guess so," he said, not seeming to give it as much thought as she was.

Delphine looked around at the booths and throngs of people browsing fresh produce, baked goods, and crafts. "I never thought the Pasadena Farmer's Market was all that beautiful, but I guess seen in the right light..."

"I meant LA, smarty pants," said Roland.

"He said you have smart pants," said Kenji, laughing.

She'd suggested they go to the Farmer's Market that afternoon, once they'd returned from downtown LA. She needed to be in a different environment to process what had gone on at the UCC, and taking a walk in the mild fall sunshine was just the ticket. Plus, she could pick up some fresh, locally grown vegetables. The drive from downtown had taken over an hour and once they'd collected Kenji, who had insisted on going along because he needed more bok choi, it was so late that some of the produce vendors were running out of things to sell and a few were beginning to pack up to leave.

The crowds were still heavy though, and at one point someone bumped into her, quite hard—enough to make her wobble for a moment. Her balance was still on point, since she practiced so much yoga and lifted weights, but it had been jarring nonetheless.

"Watch it, Grandma," said the person she'd collided with, from behind them.

"Hey!" yelled Roland, who spun to address the offender. "Don't talk to her like that!"

Delphine reached for his shoulder to stop him. "It's okay," she said. "Let it go. Happens all the time."

"But that's so mean!" said Roland, sounding incredulous.

"Old people don't have feelings, so it is okay," said Kenji.

Roland looked even more incredulous, if that were possible.

"He's pulling your leg. Of course we have feelings. We've simply become a little more used to being invisible," said Delphine.

"Sometimes it comes in handy," said Kenji.

"Absolutely," said Delphine.

"Really?" asked Roland.

Kenji said, "We can get away with all kinds of stuff."

"Huh," said Roland.

Delphine stopped in front of a crate of particularly delicious-looking carrots and pulled a reusable produce bag from her canvas market tote to load some up. "I still can't believe Sylvie wouldn't tell you who contacted her for the Beaufort," she said to Roland as the vendor weighed her selection.

"She said it would cost me," said Roland, "But I have no idea what that means."

"Right," said Kenji, sounding like he knew exactly what she'd meant.

Roland shook his head and stuck his hands into his jeans pockets. "Hey, what's this?" He pulled one hand back out, holding a slip of paper.

"How would we know?" asked Kenji. He gave Delphine another sympathetic look.

"Sylvie's number," said Roland, cringing.

Delphine smiled.

It took some convincing, but once Delphine reminded Roland that he was on assignment and working for her, and that meant he basically had to do whatever she told him to, he agreed to call Sylvie. Delphine told him what to say and how to say it, but it didn't seem like he'd been listening so she was a bit concerned he wouldn't handle it the right way.

One of her biggest flaws was not being able to give up trying to control every situation. Of course Roland would do fine—he'd had a good career as a detective up till now, and could hold his own. But still she worried.

Delphine and Kenji watched Roland pace around a lamppost as he talked on the phone.

"Do you think it will work?" Kenji asked.

Delphine paid for a bag of heirloom tomatoes and put them in her tote. "Sure."

A few minutes later, Roland came back looking like a man defeated.

"Well?" Delphine asked him.

"I have to go on a date with her," he said, sounding as defeated as he looked. "Tomorrow night."

Delphine felt bad, but really wanted him to get to the point already. "She's going to give you a name tomorrow?"

"She gave me the name just now, on the honor system, she said."

"And?"

"Gerald DeeDoo, something like that?"

Kenji and Delphine exchanged glances. "Gerard deDeiu," said Kenji. Delphine nodded.

They continued walking, past more vendors who were putting away their tables and signage.

Roland said, "He's the one who asked her for the four wheels of the … wait, what was it … Beaufort dee Alpine? But she couldn't find any."

"Beaufort d'Alpage," said Delphine in perfect French.

"Hmm," said Kenji.

"She sounds like she regrets getting involved. Back at the UCC, I asked her point blank if she was the Big Cheese and she laughed and said no."

"Do you believe her?" asked Delphine.

"Yeah, I think so," said Roland. "I think she'd like to be the Big Cheese, but she isn't. She made it sound like there isn't one anymore. Or if there is, they're being very discreet."

"Then who the heck found the cheese to put in your car?" asked Kenji.

Delphine didn't say anything as she sat down on a park bench and pulled out a small box of cookies from her grocery bag. Roland and Kenji sat down beside her and she passed out a few small, handmade Russian tea cookies. Her favorite. A local bakery, the Cookie Nookie, made the best tea cookies she'd ever tasted, and that included the ones she used to get when she was on assignment in Europe. A shame about the name of the bakery though. She winced when she closed the box and looked at the label.

"What a cool name for a bakery!" said Roland, pointing to the sticker.

Kenji snickered. "Nookie."

"Who is Gerard deDeiu?" asked Roland.

"Gerard owned a dance studio in the eighties," said Delphine. "Around the same time of our Big Cheese case, we had mandatory dance lessons as part of our training. You know, etiquette, comportment, dance. That sort of thing."

"He was a good teacher," Kenji added. He licked powdered sugar off his fingers.

"But about as sharp as a bowling ball," said Delphine.

Roland laughed, but stopped when she and Kenji gave him a look. "What? That was funny."

"It's not nice to ridicule one's shortcomings," said Kenji.

Roland hunched his shoulders. "I don't get you guys."

"I had no idea all these people were still around," said Delphine.

"Why would you?" asked Roland. "Unless you were in the cheese underworld yourself."

Delphine caught Kenji scrutinizing her, no doubt considering the possibility that she was indeed still connected to that world. "Oh please," she said, giving his shoulder a little nudge. "I'm practically lactose-intolerant these days."

They sat in silence for a moment, thinking.

"Do you think deDieu could be the Big Cheese?" Delphine asked Kenji.

"Why else would a dance instructor be asking around for fancy cheese to put in the trunk of your car?" said Roland.

"Yes, but if he is the Big Cheese, he wouldn't have had to ask Sylvie for the Beaufort," said Kenji.

"I wonder where he ended up getting it from," said Delphine.

All three of them sat in silence, perplexed.

Roland slapped his palms on the tops of his legs and stood back up. Unfortunately, he hadn't wiped the sugar off his fingers first, and now had powdery fingerprints on his thighs. "Let's go ask him ourselves."

Delphine hadn't thought of that. "Good idea!" She pulled out her phone to search on Gerard's name, but Roland put a hand out to stop her.

"No need. I know where he is."

Delphine handed him another cookie.

# CHAPTER 17

The next morning after breakfast, Delphine and Roland set off for Montrose. She let Roland drive the short distance up the 210 while she rode shotgun.

"I don't understand why he's not your partner on this, since he's always around," said Roland.

"Kenji is retired and has no desire to jump back in with both feet," she said.

"Maybe not with both feet, but he's definitely putting his nose in it."

"In the water?" asked Delphine.

"No, I mean … Never mind. He's just always around. What's the deal with you two?" Ever since he'd met Kenji, Roland had been wondering if Delphine and her former partner were more than friends. They had some sort of connection, it was clear. Roland also knew it was none of his business, but it was something to talk about as they drove.

"That's none of your business, Detective Magnusson."

Roland smiled to himself at her defensive tone; she had revealed a lot without saying much. "Maybe he should take over for me. I still don't know why I'm here," he said.

"Of course you do," said Delphine. "Kenji is a charming man, but you have a wonderful way with people and clearly Sylvie likes you. If it weren't for you, we wouldn't be on our way to see Gerard, and you wouldn't have a date tonight."

"True," he said with a touch of pride. When he'd first discovered Sylvie had slipped him her number, he'd been adamant about not calling her. But Delphine pointed out that the woman had given him her number for a reason, and Delphine declared that she wanted to know what it was. She also reminded him she was his superior and if she ordered him to make a phone call, then by golly that's what he would do.

So he'd called, and laid the charm on thick, as instructed. Sylvie said she would only reveal where the mysterious Gerald deDoo could be found if Roland agreed to meet her for a drink. He begrudgingly complied, and she revealed that the man ate breakfast every morning at the cafe he owned in Montrose. The plan had worked, and as an extra bonus—for Sylvie, anyway— they had a hot date that night.

"We're being followed," said Delphine as they passed the exit for the Jet Propulsion Laboratory, where her daughter-in-law and Zooey's mother, Zenia Puddle, worked as a mission planning systems engineer. Needless to say, the family didn't talk about work around the dinner table very often.

"I noticed that," said Roland, his eyes darting to the rearview mirror. A late-model, Nissan Sentra with faded-maroon paint trailed them in their lane, several car lengths back. Whoever was following them was good enough to be subtle, but not good enough to avoid detection.

"Impressive," said Delphine, sounding impressed.

"That someone is following us, or that I noticed?" he asked.

"Both, I guess." She craned her neck to check the side mirror. "I don't recognize the car, and I can't see inside. Too much glare."

"I can't see either." Roland looked at the map on the car's in-dash monitor. "But who the heck would even try to tail someone in a dinky car like that!"

"Someone either very confident or very stupid," said Delphine.

"Either way, we're going to lose them. Hang on." Roland hit the accelerator with a little extra force and was rewarded with an instant response from the Mercedes. His surprise subsided and a devilish grin came over his face as he settled in behind the wheel.

"Don't have *too* much fun," said Delphine, watching the road with an eagle eye.

Roland laughed as he wove in and out of freeway traffic at a speed well over the limit. He passed right by Ocean View Boulevard, the exit they were supposed to take. There was only one thing he loved more than tailing vehicles, and that was trying to lose a tail.

"Zooey wants me to get an electric car," Delphine said, reaching for the suicide handle above the passenger window. "I know I should, but I just love this car too much."

"I can see why," said Roland. "But some EVs are pretty fast too."

"Meh," said Delphine.

"Maybe one day Zooey will understand the joy that a Mercedes can bring," he said. "Till then, remind her to eat less meat. That has a greater impact on her carbon footprint."

Delphine swung her head to look at him with surprise. "Did you learn that from your wife?" she asked.

"What, can't a guy care about the environment?" Roland felt defensive. Because of course Delphine was correct.

He continued speeding up the 210, keeping an eye on the rearview mirror. The car was still behind them.

"Da—crap!" he said, and swerved to the right so hard that Delphine leaned way over to the left and almost bumped against the driver's seat. But she didn't say a word.

The Mercedes flew across two lanes of traffic and up the steep offramp for La Crescenta Avenue. The dashboard map kept glitching as it tried to reroute the trip, but at the moment directions to Montrose didn't matter. At the top of the hill he took a right turn, drove a block, and then turned right again, onto a side street where he came to a screeching stop, perfectly parked in front of a well-maintained Craftsman home. A man in his pajamas stood in the yard with a tiny white dog on a leash. The man stared at them, open-mouthed, and Delphine gave him a little wave. The dog yapped at the car until the man dragged it back inside.

"Don't you just want to punt tiny dogs like that?" said Roland, turning off the engine.

"No, not really."

They sat in silence for a few beats, collecting themselves.

"That was some driving," Delphine said, finally letting go of the suicide handle.

"It looks like we lost them," said Roland, experiencing more *Hawaii Five-0* déjà vu. "Any idea who that was?

Delphine closed her eyes in thought. "No, but something about that car was familiar. I can't quite place it though."

"What kind of car does your pal Richard drive?"

"He drives a Jaguar."

Roland tapped the steering wheel with his fingers. "That doesn't mean he couldn't have borrowed another vehicle. And what about your friend, what's his name? Shipster."

"You are terrible with names," said Delphine.

"Hmph," said Roland. It was the truth, but it still stung.

"Anyway, Ship drives a white Buick something-or-other," she said. "That wasn't him. Yes, he could have borrowed a different car, but no way that was him. The man is a terrific dancer, but a terrible driver. He crashes into everything. He almost got us all killed in Scotland once."

"How did he manage to become a fancy Falls agent if he can't drive for sh—beans?"

"Oh, he had other skills. He was great with a gun, and at hand-to-hand combat. Plus, his uncle was one of the founders." She put a finger to her lips in thought. "I still feel like I've seen that car before somewhere."

"It'll come to you at some point."

They sat on the street for a full five minutes, waiting for any sign of the Sentra, but it appeared to be long gone.

Roland started the Mercedes, pulled away from the curb, and followed the rerouted map the rest of the way to Montrose, where he parked on Honolulu Avenue in front of the Lost Bookstore.

"You sure you want me to wait here?" he asked, turning off the car's engine.

"Yes," said Delphine. She sat stone-still in the passenger seat, mentally preparing. Her phone rang, and she pulled it out of her purse, but there was no need since the call also popped up on the car's dashboard screen. "It's Richard," she said.

"I can see that," said Roland. "Put him on speaker."

"I can never get used to this whole talking car thing," said Delphine as she reached over to the driver's side of the car and pushed a button on the steering wheel. "Hello, Richard."

"Where are you?" Richard asked.

"Getting my hair done at the beauty parlor, and then I'm off to the gynecologist. Why?"

Roland tried to stifle a laugh and succeeded, but couldn't help smiling. The old lady had it going on.

Richard paused before answering. "We were able to identify a set of fingerprints on the wheels of Beaufort d'Alpage."

"I never had any doubt that you would," said Delphine. She and Roland shared a knowing look. "And?"

"And your fingerprints are on all four rinds. Also, the wheels don't appear to have come through official channels. Only two Beauforts have come into the US in the last three months."

"Well, well," she said.

"That's all you have to say for yourself?" Richard asked.

"Would you like me to recite some poetry?"

"We need to talk in person at some point," he said.

"We can meet at my gynecologist's office. I'll text you the address, she's in Santa Monica."

"I'll be in touch, Delphine." Richard hung up.

"When you think about it," said Roland, "espionage regarding illegally obtained gourmet cheese is pretty ridiculous." Taking a step back from a situation to get perspective was always a good idea—things often looked different from a higher altitude. But damn if this situation didn't look just as weird from far away as it did from right close up.

"That is a very existential observation," said Delphine.

"Huh?"

"I said, welcome to my life."

Roland couldn't let go of the cheese angle. "Fingerprints on a rind? Is that even possible? Who would…"

"Let's see if we can find out," she said.

# CHAPTER 18

Roland got out of the car but leaned back into the door opening to talk to Delphine, who still sat motionless in the passenger seat. "You sure you'll be okay? I can handle this if you want."

She shook her head. "No. I'm fine. Sometimes it hits me how much I miss all this."

"Looking for cheese smugglers?" Roland asked, grinning.

She smiled too. "All of it."

"Yeah, well, I'd rather be having a cold beer on a tropical island, but whatever floats your boat, lady." He stood up, closed the car door, and sat on a bench in front of the bookstore, which was still closed.

Delphine got out of the car and straightened the blazer of her taupe linen pantsuit. "If I'm not back in twenty minutes, come in after me," she said, and then walked across the street to Cousin Roman's Bakery. Behind her, the Mercedes' alarm chirped softly. Roland was starting to grow on her.

Delphine knew she was being watched by Roland, but also by someone in the bakery. When she entered, she took her time making her way to the table in the front left corner of the shop and sat down next to Gerard deDieu.

Gerard, a tall, heavy-set man, sat back in his chair and eyed her as he crossed his arms across his chest. He looked about the same as he used to, except for maybe a few more age lines, grey hairs, and pounds. Maybe that last trait was what happened when you switched your profession from dance studio owner to bakery owner. Wary of the situation and what Gerard might know, she placed her purse, heavy with the weight of her .38, on the table next to her. Going into a situation stone-cold had never been on her list of favorite things to do.

Gerard's tailored suit contained not one wrinkle. Delphine had never trusted French men to begin with, but his suit made her even more suspicious.

His eyes didn't display any sign of recognition and for a moment, she wondered what she should say. "I don't know if you remember me..." she began, but that was as far as she had to go.

"How could I forget you?" he asked in a loud, baritone voice. "You were always one of my best students." He reached for her right hand and brought it to his lips, giving it a cold, wet smooch that was not soundless. For a moment, Delphine went back in time to an unfortunate assignment that had involved lying in wait for half a day in a ship's cargo hold that was stuffed to the gills, so to speak, with freshly caught fish. To this day, she still could not eat herring.

"Charming as ever, Monsieur deDieu," she forced herself to say with an alluring smile.

"Billy Bob!" snapped Gerard, waving a hand.

Within seconds a tall man dressed in white seemed to appear out of thin air at the table. "Yes, boss," he said in a quiet voice.

"Deux petits déjeuners, s'il vous plaît," said Gerard, and the man vanished.

"Now then," he said, turning to Delphine. "What brings you to my fine bakery this morning?"

"I was in the mood for some French pastries," she said.

Gerard laughed a booming laugh that she bet Roland could hear from across the street. "Always such a sense of humor with this one," he said, pointing to her for the benefit of no one.

Delphine gave him a sour smile. "Okay, you got me. I ran into Sylvie recently, and she mentioned your name. It got me thinking about the good old days." She observed his face as she spoke Sylvie's name, and detected a slight change in his features, like a small cloud crossing the path of the sun—momentarily dark, but fleeting. "We had such fun at your studio. You, me, Sylvie, and I'm sure you remember Walter Shipley, Richard Dere, and Simon Pegbottam."

"Ah yes, of course. Your little gang. I remember Walter and Simon were also quite proficient dancers. Richard and Sylvie, no."

"Are you still in touch with anyone from those days?" she asked, trying to sound upbeat and not all that interested in his response.

"That was ages ago. I did hear that Monsieur Pegbottam died under unusual circumstances, is that right?"

"I'm afraid so, yes," said Delphine.

Billy Bob came back and deposited a few items on the table. Two espressos, a platter of pastries, forks and napkins, and two clean plates. Once it was all laid out, the spread created a pleasant tableau. Delphine moved her purse a little farther away from her place setting, but kept it close and within sight.

The small cup of espresso gave off tendrils of steam and smelled delicious. The pastries looked amazing—plain croissants served with ramekins of jam, as well as chocolate and almond croissants, and apple-filled pastries. Delphine took a few seconds to mourn the passing of her dearly departed metabolism.

Gerard put an almond croissant on his plate and attacked it with a tiny fork while she watched with amusement. The dainty utensil looked wrong in his big, meaty hand and he got more crumbs on the table than he did croissant in his mouth.

"When did you sell the dance studio?" she asked, unfolding a napkin onto her lap.

"Right after you and your group of friends stopped coming," he said. Now there were a few flakes of croissant on his chin.

"There was no money to be made after that. Dancing is a dying art. Or should I say, it is a dead art."

Delphine begged to differ but decided to let the comment go for the moment. She thought back to the Big Cheese operation. Mandatory dance lessons had begun about six months before the cheese case, and continued through the investigation, but were put on hold during their Peru trip. When they got back from South America, the team had another few months of lessons, but then they stopped for good, Richard announcing they had learned enough. "Did the lessons pay you that well?" she asked.

"Non, but the money laundering did," said Gerard in his thick French accent.

Delphine's brows shot up, betraying her surprise; try as she might, she'd been too overcome to stop it from happening.

"What, you did not know about that? Huh." Gerard stopped eating and scratched his chin in confusion.

"Who paid you to launder their cash?" she asked.

"I don't know," he said, shrugging his perfectly tailored gigantic shoulders. "I can't remember when they started, but they ended when … Let me see…" He looked at the ceiling. "I suppose the payments ended about the time you took a break from your lessons. But who it was? I have no idea."

"How could that happen?" Most small-time money laundering operations she knew of were done through close relationships in tight circles. Not knowing where the cash was coming from seemed reckless and ignorant. But this was Gerard, so maybe it was plausible after all.

"We made sure we had a lot of expenses. You know, new curtains, a company car, live bands…"

"I'm not talking about how you laundered it," she said, although come to think of it, laundering money through a dance studio did seem like it would have been more challenging than, say, going through a convenience store. "I meant how could you not know who was giving you the money?"

"I was young, what did I care? Someone left me cash, and I took care of it for a fee. We communicated through notes."

"I don't suppose you have any of those notes handy," she said.

He laughed. "You think I would keep them this long? I am not quite that stupid, madame."

But he might be a *little* bit dim, thought Delphine, and maybe she'd have some fun with the situation. "Why did you say you haven't seen anyone from the old days, when I know for a fact that you contacted Sylvie recently?"

"Oh, I must have forgotten," he said, and Delphine saw that cloud cross his face again.

"Who contacted you for the cheese?"

"I don't know. I got another note."

"Same handwriting?"

"Heck to me if I know. I am no graphologist." He took a sip of his espresso.

Delphine looked at her own cup. She wanted to try it, but would it be safe? Surely Gerard would have no reason to poison her. Her overactive imagination must have gotten triggered by the car chase, which definitely hadn't been her imagination.

She decided to go for it and took a small drink of the hot espresso. Delicious. The real thing, and so far, she felt fine.

"Wasn't there a phone number in the note? How were you to contact this mystery person?" she asked.

"The note said to put a sign in the window for a lost dog if I found the cheese, and one for a lost cat if I did not find the cheese. I don't know what was to happen next."

"Why did you think to ask Sylvie for the cheese?"

"Because she knows a lot about cheese," said Gerard.

"Sounds like you see her regularly."

His eyes went wide. "Oh. We, uh … from time to time…"

"Do you think Sylvie is the Big Cheese?" she asked.

"The what?" He reached for a pain au chocolat and tossed it onto his plate.

Delphine tried to remember the advice Kenji had given her the day before when she'd decided to meet up with Gerard. She had plenty of experience with extracting information, but strong-arming was usually her method of choice, not peaceful questioning. Give her a sharp enough pencil and she could get anyone to spill the beans. Kenji had always been better at what she dismissed as "talk therapy," and both he and Roland insisted on keeping things as nonviolent as possible. Sissies.

"Don't BS me," she said, placing her cup a little too forcefully back on its saucer.

"What BS?"

"You're in on the cheese dealing, don't tell me otherwise."

Gerard looked at her like she was a simpleton. That was rich, she thought.

"You are very beautiful when you are arguing," he said with a pastry-flaked smile.

Why was it that some men believed trying to charm the pants off every woman they met was some sort of sport? It was pathetic. She made a note to have a talk with Roland later, about never, ever making the same mistake. It would be a matronly, I'm-giving-you-sound-worldly-advice type of chat.

"Le Grande Fromage," she tried again, enunciating each syllable.

"This is a foreign concept to me," he said, and pulled off one end of the chocolate-filled croissant and shoved it in his mouth.

"Are *you* le Grand Fromage?"

"I have a cheese pastry, if you would like to try it? Billy Bob!"

Billy Bob materialized, but Delphine shooed him away and kept at her quarry.

"I never said that you were le Grande Fromage," said Delphine.

"I … What? I hope this is some kind of joke!" Gerard spewed crumbs as he spoke.

"Hope is the mother of fools," she said to Gerard.

Gerard picked up the tiny fork and pointed it at her. "What are you saying about my mother!"

"She's not le Grande Fromage, is she?"

"What?" he asked.

"Is she French?"

"My mother or the Big Cheese?"

"The Big Cheese." Delphine was closing in.

"No, he is not French, this Big Cheese!" Gerard slammed his baby fork on the table.

"So it's a man!"

"What is a man?"

"Is it you?"

"Non! Wait a moment…"

Delphine continued her volley. "Your mother is a man!"

"This is preposterous."

"That your mother is le Grande Fromage?"

"She is not!"

"Then who is?"

"Who is my mother?"

"Yes! Who is the Big Cheese!"

Silence.

Delphine took a small sip of her espresso. She would have to wrap this up; otherwise, they might still be going at it by the time the lunch crowd rolled in. She'd hoped for entrapment, but it seemed the cost to her own sanity to continue this tack was too high. She should have met him someplace private and used her strong-arm tactics, phooey on Kenji and Roland for insisting on no violence. It was time to pursue another line of inquiry.

She picked up a pain au chocolate from the platter, wrapped it in a napkin, and put it in her purse as she walked to the door, hoping not to get crumbs in the chambers of her pistol.

"Wait!" said Gerard right as she got to the front of the shop.

Delphine turned to see him standing next to the table, crumbs all down the front of his suit.

"Wait right there for one moment." He motioned for her to stay put and walked away in that jaunty step that European men seemed to have mastered. When he got to the back of the bakery, he disappeared behind a swinging door.

"This better be worth it," she said under her breath.

Delphine moved out of the way so a young man and a little girl could enter the bakery. They went up to the counter, and the girl's face lit up as she looked at all the French pastries on the other side of the glass. Delphine smiled. Young children had such a sense of unbounded joy. Where did that go? She sighed and looked out the front windows. Roland still sat on the bench in front of the bookstore, but now he held a cup of coffee. He gave her an inquisitive look, and she shook her head. She was fine.

"I don't know if this will help," said Gerard from alarmingly close by. He shoved a folded piece of paper at her.

Delphine took the paper but when she tried to unfold it, he put a hand on hers to stop her.

"Not here," he said. "Just in case someone is watching. I can tell you that it is not the same handwriting as the notes from years ago. It is so curious—the whole thing is the same, but different."

Normally Delphine would scoff at such an inane phrase. But in this case, she knew what he meant. She nodded her thanks and left the shop, looking back once to catch a glimpse of the *Lost Cat!* flyer in the window before crossing the street.

# CHAPTER 19

"Are you ready for your date yet?" Delphine's voice drifted down the hallway and into the guest bedroom, where Roland lay on the bed staring at the ceiling. His vision blurred with memories from his junior prom, his mom yelling at him to get downstairs because Geraldine, his date—and the bespectacled, beak-nosed daughter of his father's business partner—was waiting. Yes. This felt just like that.

"Roland?" Delphine knocked on the door and when he still didn't respond, it opened a few inches. "It's almost time to leave. Is that what you're wearing?"

He sat up. "I think you need to trust me with some things. I know women, okay?" Roland had put on his best-fitting T-shirt and the darker of his two pairs of jeans, and even cleaned his Doc Martens.

Delphine sat down on the bed. "I'm sure you do. But I know espionage."

"It'll be fine." He stood up and reached for his wallet on the dresser. "Why can't I take your car?"

"Because I want to be there. Don't worry, we won't be obvious." She got up from the bed and walked down the hall.

"We?" he called after her.

When Roland came into the living room, Kenji sat on the couch reading a newspaper.

"Ready, princess?" Kenji asked him.

"Why does he have to go?" Roland asked Delphine.

Kenji laughed. "Oh, I'm not going."

Roland put his hands on his hips. "Then why are you here?"

"Moral support. And to take pictures of you with your corsage."

The doorbell rang. Delphine said, "We are taking someone with us though."

The door opened before Delphine could get to it, and in waddled a bowlegged woman, about the same age as Kenji and Delphine, wearing a powder-blue polyester pantsuit and big librarian glasses that must've been from the '80s.

"Let's go drinking!" the woman bellowed. Then she noticed Roland standing open-mouthed in the center of the room. "Hello, what have we here?" She sidled over to him and extended her hand. "Frances Flance, attorney, and the Southland's leading expert on how to have a good time." She winked at him.

Roland shook her hand, which was large and strong. Her fingers looked gnarled with arthritis, but that didn't stop her from cutting off the circulation in his pinky.

Still clutching Roland's fingers with her right hand, she tucked a business card into the front pocket of his jeans with her left. "Call me. Let's do lunch."

It was as if there wasn't enough air in the room for anyone else to speak, and they all remained quiet as Frances walked up to Kenji. "Still single, K-man? Great, call me sometime and we'll do dinner. I'll need some sustenance after lunch with that tall drink of water." She jerked a thumb in Roland's direction.

Kenji smiled but still said nothing.

"Hello, Frances," said Delphine.

"Delphine!" Frances her arms out for an embrace. Delphine obliged. "You keep collecting hot guys. You'll have to tell me your secret."

Delphine reddened. "Yes, well, I think we'd better go."

Roland felt a tad embarrassed too. Over the last few days, the average age of the women who thought he was hot seemed to be skewing toward seventy. He kept quiet as the three of them headed to the kitchen, then into the garage to get into the Mercedes.

"Bye, kids," Kenji called from the living room. "Make responsible choices!"

Delphine dropped the keys into Roland's hand and smiled. He got to drive! At least the evening had one redeeming quality so far.

Roland backed the car out while Delphine programmed an address into the car's GPS. Sylvie had texted him a street address after he'd told her he had no idea where to meet, and he'd given it to Delphine. During the twenty-minute drive, Delphine asked Frances about her latest court cases and most recent cruise. Frances obliged, telling them a story about a case in the Bahamas regarding an all-you-can-eat clam bar, and a cruise during which she'd slept with the judge. Or something like that. He hadn't wanted to listen very closely.

They arrived safely, without having been followed, as far as Roland could tell. He'd parked on the street across from their destination and now sat behind the wheel, engine off, staring at the sign outside the bar that read *DON HO'S TIKI PARADISE* in big neon letters. A tiki bar. In North Hollywood. Of course.

"Oh *yeah!*" said Frances. "This place is amazing! I used to come here every Tuesday. At Christmastime they put up a new sign and call it Don Ho-ho-ho's Tiki Paradise. And their holiday party is out of control! I wonder if Spike still tends bar."

"Give me a few minutes' head start," Roland said, and handed the keys to Delphine.

"Don't have too much fun without me!" said Frances from the back seat as he got out of the car.

Roland walked across the side street to the bar. "Don Ho-ho-ho," he mumbled. Fifteen years as a police officer and a detective in Florida. Trips to South America to visit his wife's family. Several vacations to Europe. He'd always liked to think of himself as a fairly well-rounded individual, but never, ever, had he experienced anything as weird as he had since arriving in LA only … three days earlier? It felt like a lifetime.

That afternoon he'd called Christina to check in, and when she answered her phone, she almost sounded surprised to realize he was still out of town. So much for that old adage about absence making the heart grow fonder. Speaking of hearts, he hadn't had the courage to tell his wife that he would be going on a date of sorts that evening. It wasn't really a date, right? It was work. Like going undercover. He wondered how far he'd be expected to go, all in the name of cheese smuggling.

As he approached the front door, he noticed it was open and an instrumental ukelele version of the song "Tiny Bubbles" wafted out, along with the smell of toasted coconut.

He waited right inside the front door for a moment. The bar seemed to be lit only by candles and some red, yellow, and blue lights strung behind the bar. A back door led to patio seating, lit by tiki torches. He began to head that way before he caught sight of Sylvie waving at him from a small circular booth just to the left of the front entrance. He took a deep breath and changed course, sliding into the vinyl bench seat across from her.

"Nice place," he said, looking at the ceiling, which was basically an indoor palapa.

Sylvie picked up her purse from the seat and slid across the vinyl until she was a foot away from Roland. Her movement was accompanied by an unusual squeaking noise, and when she came up beside him, he noticed she had on a very short leopard print skirt. In fact, everything she had on featured a leopard print, including her earrings. As she settled herself, the backs of her legs continued to squeak on the vinyl.

"Yes, it is wonderful," she said. "So Californian. I took the liberty of ordering for you."

"Great," said Roland, feeling anything but.

"You look very nice," said Sylvie. She closed her eyes and breathed in deeply. "And you smell délicieux. What is that scent?" She drew out the French word for emphasis. Roland didn't know the language but had no trouble translating.

"Dove soap."

Just then an attractive young woman wearing a tight black T-shirt brought two frozen drinks to the table. She gave Roland a knowing smile and left without a word. It took everything he had not to run after her and explain it wasn't what it looked like. Except it kind of was.

He reached for one of the icy drinks and pulled it close. The frozen liquid was light brown, and a lime wheel sat on the lip of the glass. "This looks interesting," he said, and took a big slurp from the bendy straw sticking out the top. Then another. Rum.

Sylvie watched with amusement. "You may want to slow down, my darling."

"Wow!" Roland said with wide eyes. "That is strawng! And delishew, as you say." Perhaps the evening wouldn't be a total bust. "What is this?"

"They call it a Navy Grog Slushieeeee," said Sylvie, and drew out the last vowel. Combined with her French accent, the drink name sounded all kinds of wrong. Roland needed more alcohol, so he took another gulp and got the biggest case of brain freeze he'd had since the second grade.

When he could finally open his eyes again, Sylvie's expectant face came into focus first, and then, over her left shoulder, he noticed Frances and Delphine at the bar, talking to the bartender. Time to put his plan into action. The plan he hadn't told Delphine about. It was nefarious, but if he was there to do a job, then he was going to do it, by George.

"So tell me, Sylvie, how do you know Delphine?" he asked.

"Oh, I am sure she has told you all about the case she was working on all those years ago," she said, running a finger along his forearm.

Roland smiled and removed her hand. "Why don't you tell me anyway?"

"I see, you want the whole story," she said. "Well, okay. I suppose it hurts nothing to bring certain things to light now." She put her hand on Roland's arm again, and this time he didn't remove it.

"I was the protégé of Simon Pegbottam," she said. "He brought me in on Delphine's Big Cheese case as a consultant, but that was all a ruse." She stopped to take a sip of her grog.

Roland leaned forward and propped his head in his hand, turning his body to face Sylvie. "Really," he said, as if this were the most fascinating conversation ever. And he had to admit, it was getting pretty good. Out of the corner of his eye, he saw Frances give him a thumbs-up.

"Yes, you see, Simon was le Grande Fromage."

"Really!" said Roland, his eyes going round as saucers.

"Oui."

"But this Simon character was a Falls agent. Didn't anyone notice?" he asked.

"He was that good," Sylvie explained. "Simon had them all fooled. He may have been an agent, but he was first and foremost a cheese man. He began his smuggling in the late seventies and was making a great name for himself, until the Falls got him killed."

"Uh-oh," said Roland, feeling overwhelmed by the information he was receiving and the effects of the Navy Grog Slushie. "I think this calls for food."

"I have some coming. See, here it is."

Their server appeared with another round of Navy Grog Slushies and a platter of appetizers that could have fed a small herd of horses. Fries covered with unrecognizable sauces and bits of who-knew-what, fried mushrooms, fried cheese, wontons, egg rolls, and more. It all looked like indigestion to the nth degree. He gave a weak smile to the server, who rolled her eyes at him and disappeared.

"You must be hungry," he said to Sylvie.

She laughed. "You don't know the half of it." Then she slid closer to him in the booth so that they were thigh to thigh, her hand on his knee. She worked almost as fast as the Navy Grog, he noted.

"How do you know all this about Simon?" asked Roland.

"Do we have to talk about that now? Look at all this food!"

He took her hand off his knee and gingerly placed it on the tabletop. "We can probably eat *and* talk."

Sylvie reached for a fried mushroom with one hand while the other slid back under the table and rested on his quad. "Okay," she said, and popped the food in her mouth. "But let's make this fast, oui? I have a reservation for us at the Garland down the street."

Roland wasn't sure if the Garland was a restaurant or a hotel, and he sure as heck had no intention of finding out. "You were saying? How do you know so much about this Simon guy?"

"Because he was in the process of retiring and I was to be his replacement," Sylvie announced.

"Oh wow," said Roland. He momentarily forgot about the hand on his leg and reached for some fries. He had no idea what was on them, but they tasted heavenly, in part thanks to the booze. "Man, Delphine is going to be mad."

"Yes, but not for the reason you think."

"Oh, so she'll be extra mad?"

"Things were very, very complicated," she said, and shot him a barracuda-like smile before eating another mushroom.

He conjured up his own predatory smile and began to reach for Sylvie's hidden hand again, which had begun to rub circles on his thigh and creep slowly upward. "You're going to have to do better than that," he whispered.

Sylvie removed her hand from his leg and tapped the tip of his nose with it. "You are absolutely adorable, Roland. Okay, here is the rest of the story. Are you ready?"

He nodded.

"Delphine's boss, Richard, found out about Simon and his plan for me to take over. Instead of turning us in, he tried to strike a deal with us. If I agreed to have an affair with him, he would keep quiet about the whole thing, thus allowing me to become le Grande Fromage, and for Simon to retire from all of it."

"But that kind of thing is illegal," said Roland.

Sylvie laughed. "You are so cute, and naive. I'm not proud of what I did. I mean Richard! The man looks like the Humpty Dumpty, non?"

"That's what I said!" said Roland, pointing at her with an inebriated finger.

They both burst out laughing, and when they finally stopped, Sylvie took a moment to catch her breath before continuing.

"Yes, well, it was much harder for women to get ahead back then. I would have done anything to be le Grande Fromage. And look where I ended up, after all of it. After Simon's death, Richard said if I didn't walk away from everything, he would expose me."

Roland nodded. He'd heard his mother tell stories of workplace inequalities, and it sounded as if she'd experienced many during her career as a pilot for one of the major airlines. But before he could get too far down that rabbit hole of wondering if his mom had had to sleep with someone in order to realize her dream of flying a commercial jet, he made a mental U-turn and headed back to the dangerous waters that Sylvie Lowenstein sailed in. "That must have been hard for you," he said.

"I try not to be bitter, but yes, it was. It still is. In those days, no one took women seriously. And now it feels like no one takes older women seriously."

Roland looked into her eyes and was swept up in the moment. "Some people do."

She burst out laughing. "Oh my dear, you are too sweet." She reached up and ran her fingers through his hair. Roland hoped she hadn't got any French fry grease in it.

"So Richard killed Simon and took over as the Grand Cheese," he said.

"I don't know."

"You killed Simon and took over as Grand Cheese?"

"Mon deiu. You are thick when you're drunk."

Just then, a loud burst of laughter from the bar caught their attention.

"Your friends are not very subtle," she said.

# CHAPTER 20

Roland caught Delphine's attention, and twenty seconds later she, Frances, and their tropical drinks had joined him and Sylvie in the tiny booth.

"Isn't this cozy," said Sylvie. "Hello, Delphine. And, ah, hello to whoever you are." She waved a hand in Frances' direction. Frances wiggled her fingers at Sylvie as she slurped the last of her blue drink.

"You don't seem too surprised to see them," Roland said to Sylvie.

She put her hand back on his arm again. "Do you take me for a simpleton? I have been around the street a few times. I knew you wouldn't come alone and it's not as if they are very discreet."

Delphine knew she had a very small window between the total disappearance of Roland and Sylvie's fleeting sobriety, and the point when they would slip too far into an alcoholic haze to be helpful. Normally she would caution him about getting so inebriated, but in this case perhaps it was called for, and it wasn't like he had any secrets about the case to spill.

"Sylvie," said Roland, "It sure would be great if you could tell Delphine what you were … you were … What was I trying to say?"

"You want me to tell Delphine what I told you?" Sylvie asked.

Roland snapped his fingers. "That's it!"

Sylvie let out what could only be called a drunken giggle. "Okay, sexy detective."

Frances whistled. "Whooee, Roland, you are on fire!"

He waggled his eyebrows at her, took another swig of his grog, and scooped up another handful of fries.

Delphine perused the platter of appetizers. The fried cheese looked enticing.

"Help yourself," Sylvie said, catching her eye.

Frances wasted no time reaching for a fried clam and scarfed it down. "Decent. Not as good as the seafood on my last cruise, but still good." She licked the grease off her fingers and reached for another one.

Delphine put a piece of fried cheese on a napkin, patted the grease off, and nibbled at it. She waited for Sylvie to continue, but the woman was engrossed in trying to feed Roland a French fry.

Roland caught Sylvie's hand before it made it to its intended destination and redirected it to her own mouth. "You were going to tell Delphine about Simon," he reminded her. Delphine made a note to be sure Roland got special recognition for going above and beyond the call of fried food duty.

"Delphine, I hate to tell you this, but your wonderful Simon Pegbottam was le Grande Fromage," said Sylvie.

Delphine had been about to help herself to a fry, but stopped mid-reach, frozen and flabbergasted at the nerve of Sylvie insinuating that Simon had been the original Big Cheese. He'd been a mentor to her, educating her on the finer points of imported cheese and the intricacies of the foxtrot. But the whole time he'd been running a racket? It didn't compute. "No way," she said. "Simon was a Falls agent. He wouldn't do something like that. I learned so much from him."

"Me too," Sylvie said. "I was going to take over for him once he retired, but then he was killed."

Over the next few moments, Sylvie explained Simon's long

history as the infamous cheese smuggler, her own plans for succession, and ended her monologue with the story of Richard's betrayal.

Delphine considered every word, and as much as she didn't want to believe Simon had been dealing in dirty cheese, it all seemed plausible. "Richard must have taken over himself," she said. "He must have killed Simon, covered it up, and taken everything over."

"I cannot say," said Sylvie. "I know nothing of Simon's death, and I have only been in the outer circles of the cheese underworld since that time."

"Until recently," said Roland.

Sylvie looked guilty but explained to Delphine. "I've been thinking of getting back into the business. I recently started to make inquiries."

"Yet you still weren't able to procure four wheels of Beaufort for Gerard," Delphine said.

"Correct. There does not seem to be any Beaufort anywhere right now."

Delphine tapped the tabletop with her finger. Why didn't whoever framed her simply give up on finding such an exclusive product? They must have been very, very intent on sending a message, and that message was that they wanted Delphine to take the fall for their operation.

And Richard. That horrible man! "This is all incredible. I never trusted Richard, but to find out he covered all this up…" Delphine clenched her jaw and felt her blood pressure rise. She had been hoping for insight but hadn't been ready encounter such sobering revelations.

Sylvie laughed. "Ah, perhaps you are the hornswoggled."

Frances snorted. Roland laughed but stopped when Delphine scowled at him. She did not find it funny.

"This is serious, and no laughing matter."

"But I bet you're feeling the hornswoggled," said Roland, and Frances snorted again.

"Yes, I believe I am," said Delphine, lowering her head. She rarely felt overwhelmed by situations, but this one was getting to her. Too much coming at her too fast.

"How do you suppose Gerard fits into all this?" asked Roland, trying to look at Sylvie. It was difficult since she now had her chin on his shoulder.

"You really do smell wonderful," she said in a dreamy voice.

"Roland," said Delphine, "would you mind going over to the bar and seeing what Spike wants? I think I saw him waving at us."

"Sure." He turned to Frances, who sat on his other side and was at the edge of the circular seat. "Would you excuse me?"

"You bet," said Frances. She slid out of the booth and put her purse on her shoulder. "I'll go with you. Spike is a much less complicated person than anyone at this table. And I like my bar talk simple. Like my men."

They heard her laugh at her own joke as she walked away, and Roland followed with an unsteady gait. Delphine would be driving them home—it had been her plan all along since she figured Roland would get a little tipsy.

"I will go too," said Sylvie, but Delphine put a hand on the woman's wrist.

"We're not quite done yet," said Delphine. "Look, I know you're mad that we didn't try to exonerate you all those years ago, but as you can now see, we didn't know the real story. And by the sound of it, you were performing illegal activities so in all honesty, I have nothing to be sorry about. How about you help me? Not because Roland is charming, but because it's a chance to put some of this right, after all this time."

Sylvie looked to the bar, where Roland sat with Frances. "He is charming, isn't he."

"He's married, dear," said Delphine.

Sylvie scoffed. "I'm French. That means nothing."

"Let's focus on Gerard for a moment."

"Fine," said Sylvie, crossing her arms. "Gerard laundered

Simon's cheese money back in the old days, but that was all he did. He never knew who he was doing it for."

"And you never told him?"

Sylvie looked shy. "I was very loyal to Simon. I miss him terribly."

Delphine did too, but she couldn't let emotion prevent her from getting to the bottom of all this. "Maybe Gerard wants to take control of the operation now."

Sylvie laughed. "Non, impossible. You have talked to him. You know he is not capable of taking care of such important business."

After her conversation with the man earlier that day, Delphine had to agree.

Sylvie continued. "A few weeks ago, he asked me for the wheels of Beaufort. But I believe that is where his involvement begins and ends."

"Why didn't Richard contact you himself for the cheese?" asked Delphine. The questions were still piling up.

"Ah, but you are assuming Richard is the one who wanted the cheese," said Sylvie.

"True," said Delphine as she thought about that. "But who else could it be?"

"How should I know? I think that is your job to find out, not mine."

Now a few more dots had been connected. Maybe not all, but more. Delphine ate an egg roll to help improve her concentration. Halfway through the crispy treat, she stopped. "Are you and Gerard...?"

Sylvie spoke just above a whisper and said, "Gerard is very good at three things. Dancing, French pastries, and—"

Delphine held up a hand and interrupted her. "That's all I need to know."

"We love to ... dance," said Sylvie with a smile.

Delphine leaned back in the booth, mind reeling. "Why did whoever it was go to Gerard?" She felt the beginnings of a headache coming on.

Sylvie gave a casual wave of her hand. "Oh, you know. People stick with what they know, correct? That is always easier. Or perhaps this person was simply trying to add another layer of misdirection."

Delphine needed to mull everything over before she could begin to think of what to do next. She needed to relax in a warm bath. Looking toward the bar, she said, "I think I'd better get Roland home."

They both watched as he waved his arms in the air, a look of wide-eyed determination on his face. Frances and Spike were enraptured.

"Are you sure?" asked Sylvie. "He looks like he is just getting going."

Delphine smiled as she watched Roland, but something caught her eye that was much more sobering. Sitting two tables away from her own booth was Walter Shipley, wearing sunglasses, a baseball cap, and a Hawaiian shirt. He appeared to be attempting a Jimmy Buffett impersonation while sipping from a tall frozen drink.

"Is something wrong?" asked Sylvie.

"Do you remember Walter Shipley?"

"Oh yes, he was a very good dancer. Also a bit of a player, non? I seem to recall he hit on anything with breasts."

Delphine laughed. That was an accurate assessment. "Yes, well, he hasn't changed much. And he's sitting right over there." She rested a hand on the table and pointed her index finger at Shipley's table.

Sylvie had the presence of mind not to crane her neck and gawk. Instead, she placed her elbow on the table and rested her chin in her hand. Her eyes slid in the direction Delphine had indicated. "Well, will you look at that," she said. "What does it mean?"

"I don't know. I wonder if someone sent him here, or…"

"Could he be the Big Cheese?"

"I suppose it's possible." Delphine's spine went rigid. "Oh my goodness, maybe so! He was there at the cheese shop the day Simon was killed." Her heart felt like it skipped a beat. What if…

"Should we send him a drink?"

"No," said Delphine. "I have a better idea."

# CHAPTER 21

Delphine and Sylvie slid into the booth on either side of Ship.

"Hello, Shipley," said Delphine.

A look of surprise came over his face, but Delphine could tell it was fake. But when his expression turned to guilt with a hint of trepidation, she knew *that* was real.

"Oh my goodness, Delphine, I had no idea you were here!"

"And what about me?" said Sylvie from his other side.

Ship jumped an inch off the bench seat and spun to look at her. "Sylvie? Wow, I didn't recognize you!"

Delphine watched as sweat broke out on his cheeks and he pushed the sunglasses farther up his nose. "How can you recognize anyone with those glasses on?" she asked.

"Haha, right, I can't see a thing, haha," Ship said.

Delphine glanced over at the bar. Roland was watching them and looked like he might spring out of his chair at any second, but she pursed her lips to try and indicate she didn't need his help. He nodded once.

"What're you doing here, Ship?" she asked.

"Oh you know, just catching the ball game." He looked up at the wall behind the bar, but there was no TV there, or anywhere else in the room. "I mean, I was on my way home to catch the game. Yeah, that's it."

Sylvie leaned over the table to look at Delphine. "He is still a terrible liar," she said. Delphine nodded.

"I guess I'd better be on my way!" Ship popped up to his feet and scurried for the front door.

"What was that about?" asked Sylvie.

"I don't know," admitted Delphine. "Maybe he wanted to find out what we were talking about. I hope we weren't too loud."

They were silent and listened to the music playing in the bar—an exotic, almost creepy song, complete with bird squawks and monkey chatter. It took Delphine back to an assignment in the jungles of Belize and made her wish she had mosquito repellent in her purse.

"If he heard anything over this music, it would be a miracle," said Sylvie. "Besides, he probably wasn't here long, or you would have noticed sooner."

Delphine hoped Sylvie was right, but there was no way to know, and she felt bad about not having kept a better eye on her surroundings. "It's time to leave. I need to think."

"Take a bath," said Sylvie. "That always works best for me."

"Me too."

"Just do me one favor," said Sylvie.

Delphine was apprehensive, but curious. "What's that?"

"If you plan to do anything, I would like to help."

"Why Sylvie, I have no idea what you mean." Delphine smiled slid out of the booth. "But okay."

Delphine went to the bar and collected her wards, which was difficult since Roland was still telling stories.

"...And then you'll never believe where I found the dolphin," he said.

Spike's eyes were as big as saucers. "Where?" He rested his chin on his burly knuckles.

"Well, see, that's the thing," began Roland, apparently about to launch into another monologue.

But Delphine ran out of patience first. "Roland, you'll have to come back and finish the story for your new friend some other time. We have to get going." She wrapped her fingers around his arm and pulled him off the barstool.

"Whoa!" said Roland, steadying himself. "You're strawng!"

"Still practicing your log rolling, Delphine?" asked Frances, and Roland burst out laughing.

"Okay, let's go. Bye, Spike," said Delphine.

"Bye, guys!" Spike waved as they left.

Outside, Delphine breathed the somewhat fresh LA night air and sighed it out.

They walked to the car in silence until Roland stage-whispered, "The Sentra!" and pointed at a old maroon car parked under a streetlight, several cars down from the Mercedes.

He took a step toward the mystery car, but Delphine, who was still holding him by the arm, kept him back. "Wait," she said. They stopped at the curb of the side street.

Delphine squinted, as if that would help to see into the car, but it was too far away to see much detail. There were two occupants, however—that much she could make out. The one in the passenger seat ducked down too fast for her to tell who it was. But the driver, on the other hand, was staring right at her.

Clear as day, Delphine caught sight of two sparkly shimmers in the darkness. Mitzi Bouffant's dangly, sparkly earrings. The shimmers disappeared below the dashboard.

"This is exciting!" said Frances, for once in a quiet voice. "Let me find my gun!" She began to riffle through her bag.

"For the love of Pete, Frances, no!" whispered Delphine.

"Who is it?" asked Roland in his not-quiet voice.

"Ship and Mitzi," said Delphine.

"Ohhhhhh," said Roland, probably thinking close to the same thing she was.

Mitzi must have been the one who'd been driving when she and Ship tailed the Mercedes down the 210. Not a bad bit of driving, actually. "I guess when we were tailed, I missed the sparkle from the earrings due to the glare on the windshield."

"Well, I wanna go over there and congratulate Miffy on her excellent automobileshipness the other day," said Roland.

Delphine let go of his arm. "You do that."

Roland gingerly stepped off the curb and headed for the Sentra. But before he got halfway there, the Sentra's engine started up and the car zoomed down the street, taking the turn onto Vineland Avenue at a dangerous speed yet with precision.

"Definitely not Ship driving," said Delphine.

They piled into the Mercedes and arrived back in Pasadena right before ten. Kenji was waiting for them at the kitchen island, reading a book. Delphine couldn't read the title but judging by the cover art, it was some sort of spy thriller. Maybe he did miss the old days just a little.

Delphine made sure Roland got into bed to sleep off the Navy Grog Slushies, and when she came out to the living room, Kenji handed her a mug of herbal tea.

"None for you, Frances?" she asked her friend, who sat at the island, mugless.

"I've got to be getting home. I have a friend coming over later and then a court case in the morning. Copyright infringement waits for no one."

"The life you lead," said Kenji with wonder in his voice.

Frances tossed her keys in the air, catching them with a practiced hand. "You bet your bippie! My mind is still sharp as a tack and all those cruises don't pay for themselves." Then she turned serious. "Delphine, we've been best friends for a million years now, and I've watched you take on some dangerous people and live through some precarious situations. But this is different." She stopped to gesture to the three of them in turn. "We are all still amazing people, but we aren't thirty anymore. Heck, we're not fifty anymore. If this guy Richard wants to make you take the fall for something, it might be easier for him to push you off that ledge now than it used to be."

Delphine was not a hugger, but if she were to hug anyone, it would be Frances. She also didn't take criticism well from many people; however, she always listened to her best friend. Everyone should be so lucky to have a Frances in their lives, she thought. "I appreciate your concern, Francie. I know we're not as … robust as we used to be, but we still have a few advantages."

"Yeah!" said Kenji, raising his steaming mug.

"Anyway," said Frances, tossing her keys again, "if you plan anything big, I wanna be there."

Delphine shrugged. "I'd don't know that it will be *big*."

Frances laughed. "I know you, D. You live large. You can count on me if you need some backup or whatever. It's been ages since I've played cops and robbers."

"You just said Delphine should be very careful," said Kenji. "Why would you yourself want to do something potentially dangerous at your advanced age?"

"Because, K-Man, I'm a thrill-seeker." She waggled her eyebrows at him and shuffled out the door.

"I like her," said Kenji.

"Me too," said Delphine.

Delphine filled Kenji in on the events of the evening, after which he was very quiet, thinking over everything that had come to light. She needed to do the same. She sent him home with the understanding that the next day, she and Roland would come up with a plan, and Kenji would serve as adviser. Then she took a nice hot bath and went to bed.

# CHAPTER 22

"I admit I was skeptical, but this feels really good," said Roland. He wiggled his toes in the little tub of warm, milky-looking water. A foot soak under the pergola was the perfect way to recover from the previous evening's excitement.

"Yes," agreed Delphine. "Kenji, you'll have to share this amazing foot soak recipe."

"Ancient Japanese DIY," Kenji said. "Good for not thinking too much."

"That would explain a lot about the lack of progress on this case," said Roland.

Delphine ignored his gripe. "Not thinking too much is the key to finding a good solution," she said. "Let's not think of how to expose the Big Cheese."

They were silent again, enjoying the beautiful weather and the amazing foot soak. A few moments later, Roland felt himself being shaken awake.

"Was I snoring?" he asked, and Delphine nodded. "Sorry. I guess I'm still a little tired from last night."

"And you're sure you don't remember anything past Shipley showing up?" she asked.

Roland rubbed his temples. "No."

Delphine let out a barely audible single chuckle.

He scowled at her, unsure of whether she was giving him a hard time for not being able to recall the latter part of the evening, or implying that he had done something memorable and possibly embarrassing. He wouldn't put it past her to tease him. But then again, try as he might, the events of the evening would not come back to him. "What time did we get back here?"

"Oh, I think it was around one thirty by the time we found you and got enough clothes back on you to put you in the car," she said.

"Okay, now I *know* you're pulling my leg," he said.

"She sent me pictures," said Kenji, and Roland rubbed his temples again.

Delphine had woken him up at eight that morning, and the day had gotten off to a questionable start. What had been in those diabolical slushies? He was pretty sure Sylvie had bought him at least three, and he really should have stopped after one. But it seemed like a good idea at the time, like so many bad ideas often did. The rest of the evening was probably lost forever.

In any case, he'd felt terrible upon waking, but Delphine made him drink several glasses of water and eat a very light breakfast and threatened him with bodily harm if he didn't attend yoga with her. And wouldn't you know it, he felt a lot better now, just sleepy after a light lunch and a foot soak. He'd enjoyed the yoga class more than he thought he would. Maybe he'd continue with it when he got back home. Maybe.

"Don't tell my wife about it," said Roland.

"What?" asked Delphine.

"Did I say that out loud?" he said, feeling self-conscious. Why had that come out of his mouth?

"Are you referring to this foot soak?" she asked.

"I guess. And yoga. If she finds out I like this sh—tuff, she'll make me go to the spa with her or something ridiculous like that."

"Don't you want to do things with your wife?" asked Kenji.

"Sure," he said. But it didn't sound convincing, even to his own ears. The truth was, things hadn't been all that great for a while. He avoided the issue by working all the time, and she avoided it by not talking to him on the occasions he was home. He vowed to try harder when he got back.

"He doesn't have to talk about his personal life with us, Kenji," said Delphine. "Roland went above and beyond in getting intel from Sylvie, so cut him some slack."

"Fair enough," said Kenji. "You could do worse," he told Roland.

"I'm married!" Roland said.

"Eh," said Kenji.

Roland winced. "She's already texted me three times. Says I owe her another date."

Delphine dismissed him with a wave. "We'll send Kenji on that assignment."

Kenji's eyes grew wide, and Roland laughed. "You could do worse," he said.

From there the conversation devolved into bickering about past assignments, who owed who what, and the question of exactly what ingredients comprised Kenji's amazing foot soak recipe.

Finally Delphine held up her hands. "Let's just circle back around to what's next, shall we?"

They removed their feet from the heavenly water and dried them off. Delphine offered Roland some lotion—unscented, but still Roland declined. Moisturized feet? He was already on the verge of not recognizing himself.

"You are going after Richard?" Kenji asked.

Delphine nodded. "He makes me so mad," she said and slammed her small fist on the arm of her wicker patio chair.

Kenji turned to her. "Are you mad because of what he did back then or because you didn't catch it?"

Delphine's head snapped in his direction. "Does that matter right now? Honestly, we don't need your philosophizing, Kenji."

Kenji's lips drew into a tight line, and he closed his eyes again.

Roland smiled; they acted like an old married couple, despite their insistence there was nothing between them. Maybe that's how it was with old friends. He hoped he had a friendship like that by the time he got to their age.

"I need time to think some more," said Delphine. "Roland, Kenji is going to show you around town for a little while. Then we will meet back up later this afternoon."

"Don't you want my input?" asked Roland.

"This is how she works," said Kenji. "She will figure out what she wants to do, then she will ask you. Do not question the ways of the jedi."

Delphine stood up. "Okay, when you start quoting *Star Wars*, it's time to break up the party."

Roland and Kenji helped clear the patio of tea mugs and soaking tubs, all the while doing Yoda impressions and shouting, "It's a trap!" in their best Admiral Ackbar voices at Delphine, who seemed to do her level best to ignore them until they left.

Kenji took Roland on a driving tour of Pasadena, showing him the Rose Bowl, Old Town, and the Huntington Library—one of Kenji's favorite places. Then they stopped at Vromans, a famous local bookstore, for a coffee and to browse. Roland wondered why he was visiting so many bookstores on a work assignment, but maybe it was … a sign from the universe that he should read more?

They walked around the store, lingering at the gifts and stationary section, where Kenji watched all the ladies who browsed the pens and tote bags and notebooks. From there they headed to the mystery section, at Roland's insistence.

"Why did you bring me to this place?" he asked Kenji.

"Four reasons," said Kenji. "We needed a break, they have good coffee, there are cute ladies in the stationery section, and also so you can get a book for your wife."

"My wife?" asked Roland, who was just glad Kenji hadn't said anything about receiving a sign.

"You said your wife likes to read."

Had he said that? Kenji had an annoyingly good memory. They turned down the aisle at the beginning of the alphabet.

"Tell me," said Roland, "why are you so interested in my personal life? What's it to you? We don't know each other."

"Maybe I am trying to get to know you," said Kenji. Then he shrugged. "Maybe that is what happens when you retire."

"You get too nosy?"

"No, you want everyone to be as happy as you are."

"So you're happy, huh?"

Kenji stopped in front of the Raymond Chandler books and Roland watched as his expression turned from thoughtful to crestfallen. "I suppose. But I see now that you don't have to wait this long to experience real happiness," he said.

Roland got the message. He picked out a mystery book for himself and had one of the employees help him pick out a book for Christina from the fantasy section. She loved all that dragon stuff. When he paid for everything, he added a tote bag to his purchase.

"Have you heard from Delphine?" asked Roland as they walked to Kenji's car.

Kenji shook his head. "But don't worry. I can tell a plan is formulating in her stunningly clever mind, but she needs quiet. Are you sure you don't want to go back to the Huntington Library? The gardens are stunning."

"Nah," said Roland. The truth was, he'd gotten far enough outside his comfort zone with the yoga and the foot soak, and also that fake date. And if he went any farther, he might not make it back into familiar territory. On second thought, maybe that wouldn't be so bad. But still, no gardens.

"Can we get into the cheese market? I saw some things there that I might like to try."

"In the lounge, or the market?" asked Kenji, smiling.

"Both?"

"We cannot make it there and back in time for early dinner. Too much traffic."

"It's probably just as well I cut down on dairy. All this food plus the alcohol…" He patted his belly, which was thankfully still fairly flat.

Kenji said, "We have to stay local. The Huntington is right down the street."

"No gardens."

"Fine. Let's go to the Super Target across the street and look at office supplies."

An hour-and-a-half later, the two men arrived back at Delphine's with dinner—fresh, delicious pho from Kenji's favorite Vietnamese restaurant. Tasty and not too bad for you, Kenji had said. Roland made sure to get the vegetarian version.

As they ate, they chatted about Roland's observations about Pasadena, and Kenji informed Delphine of what office supplies were on sale at Target.

Once their meal was done, Delphine pushed her chair away from the table but didn't stand up. "Zooey would give me such a hard time about all this packaging," she said.

Roland looked at the table. Pint containers had held the broth, and the fresh vegetables and noodles had come in cardboard clamshells. Cilantro and lime wedges were packaged in small bags. "Wow," he said. "That is a lot of waste."

"Pfft," said Kenji. "This restaurant uses biodegradable materials. We will outlast those containers."

"Oh," said Delphine, sounding relieved. "Zooey will be happy to know that."

"Plus, it is the best pho," Kenji added.

"It was very good," said Roland. "So Delphine, do you have a cunning plan?"

"Maybe," said Delphine.

"She does," confirmed Kenji, and he pointed at her. "I know that look of hers."

Delphine had baked them some cookies that afternoon, and she brought out a plate piled high with her signature chocolate chip masterpieces. She explained her plan to them. Neither man spoke until she had finished outlining the entire thing, and each had eaten at least three cookies.

"That sounds pretty good," said Kenji.

"What is Kenji's role?" asked Roland.

"I'm not going," said Kenji. "Remember, I am only an adviser." He looked at Delphine with a mix of what Roland guessed was concern and regret.

"I understand," she said. "You're being smart. I'm getting out after this as well."

"I thought you said it was like *The Godfather*?" asked Roland.

Then came more imitations, jokes about cannoli, and again Delphine appeared disinterested.

"Well, I guess it's up to you and me then," Roland said to her. "I don't usually do these types of operations, but maybe it'll be fun. How dangerous could it be? We're talking cheese after all."

"Kenji and I have been doing this kind of work for a long time," she said. "And the most important rule is to never underestimate anyone or any situation. The more innocent the subject seems, the more unpredictable things can be."

# CHAPTER 23

Delphine stood in front of the mirror in her bedroom, making a few last-minute adjustments to her gown—a jade-green vintage dress that was formfitting, but cut in such a way that she could still move freely and wear her pistol in her ankle holster. It would've been nice to have the weapon in a handier location but wearing it on her ankle was better than not having it with her at all. She hoped she wouldn't have to use it at the Sassy Steppers Dance Studio, but one couldn't be too careful.

Some days she still felt sentimental about her old job, wishing she could be part of the action, wishing she could still make a difference and have a little excitement in her life. But other days, like today, Delphine knew in her heart that it was time to move on. There were other adventures waiting for her out there. Somewhere.

But first, she needed to put her plan into action. And tonight at the Trotting Foxes' regular Monday night open-studio meetup would be the perfect time. If she was right, everyone would be there, and it would be the best opportunity to close this chapter of her life. That wasn't to say the thrill of the game wasn't fun, or that a small part of her longed for some *real* excitement. But it was time to clear her name. Time to find out who the real Big Cheese was … if there was one at all…

Once Kenji had left with Roland to go out on the town the day before, she'd had another foot soak and mug of tea, and made a few calls to put some non-cheese wheels in motion. After dinner she and Roland had finalized the plan, and now it was time to go.

Delphine smoothed her dress one last time and went out to the living room, where of course Kenji was waiting to see them off. She caught his eye, and they shared a look. She realized she'd been wishing for many things when it came to her former partner, and in that moment, she knew none of those wishes would come true. He looked almost apologetic, and she nodded at him and looked away. This was no time for sentimentality.

Roland emerged from the kitchen wearing a dark-blue suit that fit him like a very well-tailored glove. Kenji had taken him shopping on their outing, and Delphine was pleased with the result.

"I know, right?" said Roland, brushing the front of the suit jacket. "I look fantastic."

She smiled; it was true. "Now you'll have something you can take on all your secret assignments," she said with a tiny bit of regret since she wouldn't be there to see him fight crime looking so good.

"Let's see how this one goes before we start planning his future," said Kenji.

"Do you have your weapon?" she asked Roland.

He nodded and patted his jacket under his left arm.

"I put the fruit punch in your trunk," said Kenji.

Delphine clasped her hands together. "Oh, thank you. I couldn't bear another night of that—"

"Bilge water?" said Roland.

"Precisely," she said. "Well, we'd better get going."

"Remember to keep your friends close and your enemies closer," Kenji said to Roland.

"I am one with the force and the force is with me," said Roland, and Kenji saluted him.

Thirty minutes later, Roland parked Delphine's E350 in the lot in front of the dance studio. No front-row spot in front of ScriptDoctor tonight; the whole strip mall was packed.

"Are all these people here for dancing?" he asked.

"Some," said Delphine. "But I think ScriptDoctor has open office hours one night a week. And it's possible that the bar in the laundromat offers karaoke on Mondays."

"This town is amazing," said Roland.

"It's just as strange as Miami," she pointed out.

"Yeah, but … I don't know. It's different. I like it better out here, I think."

Delphine smiled. "I've been around the world several times over and have seen a lot. I would say that all large cities are the same, but I know what you mean. I do like this place, which is why I've called it home my whole life, up till now."

"Do you think about leaving?"

"Oh, I don't know. If I make it out of this situation, maybe I should think about it. Have an adventure or two that might be a smidge less dangerous."

Roland nodded. "Yeah," he said. He ran one hand across the polished wooden steering wheel of the Mercedes. "Maybe I should get one of these," he said absently. "Oh, who am I kidding. My wife would never approve. Too flashy, she would say."

"They're gas guzzlers anyway," said Delphine. She reached down and adjusted her ankle holster again.

"Got your gun?" he asked her.

She nodded. "And everything else. Go ahead and start recording."

"Are you sure that's necessary? It seems a little over the top."

Delphine turned to face him and gave him a hard look. Then she shook her head. They'd all gone soft, these cops. "In my world there is no such thing as over the top. Turn it on."

"Yes, boss." He pulled out his phone from the inside pocket of his coat, fired up the recording app, and put the phone back.

Delphine reached over and adjusted the tiny Bluetooth mic that she had secured to the underside of his jacket lapel earlier. "Perfect." Her own small recording device was tucked discreetly into her bra and had been turned on when she'd gotten dressed. It was voice activated—a little fancier than the one she had provided for Roland.

Roland adjusted the sleeves of his shirt under the coat jacket as they walked toward the dance studio and stopped once to retie one of his Doc Martens.

"Are you nervous?" asked Delphine as she watched him squirm.

"Nah," he said, but she could tell he hadn't quite convinced himself. "I just hope I remember some of the dance steps Marvis taught me."

"You can make stuff up, it'll be fine," said Delphine. She'd spent an hour earlier in the day trying to coach him, but it had been hopeless.

She hooked her arm in his as they got closer to the door.

"You look lovely," Roland said as he eyed her floor-length gown.

"For an old lady?"

"Any guy over seventy would be lucky to have you as his date."

Delphine gave him the evil eye until he added, "Any guy over thirty."

# CHAPTER 24

Delphine and Roland stood inside the door, still arm in arm. She took a quick inventory of the room and then led Roland to one of the round folding tables on the far side of the studio that had been set up to accommodate the larger than usual crowd. Franko must have done some promoting to get more people in the door. It was good for business, but maybe not so good for her plan.

Marvis sat between her husband Franko and Walter Shipley, and waved as Delphine and Roland approached. Next to Marvis sat Judy Espinoza, Richard's assistant. Delphine gave her a knowing look, and Judy smiled and turned away.

That evening at dinner, Kenji told Delphine that he'd done some investigating into where Judy's loyalty might be. And by investigating, he meant taking her to coffee that morning. She told him it had been her intention to help Delphine and not set her up, as they'd feared. Judy detested Richard Dere and wanted to see him fail. And when Kenji had told her they were trying to take him down, she'd asked if she could be there to watch. Delphine believed the story and invited Judy to come to the studio that evening. Perhaps she would ask the shy woman to officially join the Foxy Trotters.

At the same time, Mitzi Bouffant was approaching the table

from a different direction, and it looked like they all might end up colliding.

"Saved you a seat, babe!" said Shipley, pulling out the chair next to him without getting up.

When Mitzi realized he was beaming at Delphine and not her, she huffed loudly and course corrected, aiming for the refreshments table.

Roland and Delphine stopped in front of the table and Roland pointed at Ship. "Is this the dance partner you were telling me about?" he asked Delphine.

"He is," she said.

Roland glowered at Ship. "I see."

Ship looked part crestfallen, part nervous. Interesting. She took the seat he offered her, and Roland sat on her other side, turning his chair away from the group a bit so he had a better view of the room.

"Let's get this party started!" said a voice a few feet from the table. Frances waddled up and sat down in the last available chair, letting out an involuntary "Umph!" as she hit the seat. Then she looked at Roland. "Young man, can I hire you as my personal companion?"

"No thank you, ma'am," said Roland. "I'm already gainfully employed."

"How much is Delphine paying you? I'll give you double. Plus Tuesdays off." Frances pulled her billfold out of her purse and handed him a twenty. "Go get me a plate of snacks, would you?"

Roland looked at Delphine for help. "You should consider it," she told him. "Frances is loaded."

When Roland made no move to get up, Frances snatched her twenty from his hand and put it back in her wallet. "Your loss," she said.

"So, you and Mitzi?" Delphine said to Shipley.

Now he looked guilty. "I was going to tell you," he said.

"I should hope so." Delphine still wasn't sure what he might be talking about—dancing or romance. Probably both.

"It's just that, well, I know you and I have won a lot of trophies together, but don't you think maybe it's time for a change?"

"But Delphine, what about the regional competition next month?" asked Marvis, who had been listening to their conversation.

"I want to win," Delphine said to her, "but I don't want to win *that* badly." She turned to look at Ship. "Besides, we don't want things to get stale, do we? Probably time for both of us to branch out."

She put a hand on Roland's arm.

Roland, who had been watching the activity in the room, leaned over to her and said, "What's that, babe?"

The word produced the exact reaction she'd hoped for from Ship.

"We could discuss it," Ship said, backpedaling. "I mean, nothing is set in stone." He gave her a weak smile.

"No, that's okay. You're right, time to move on."

"But wait!" said Ship, looking at Roland with jealousy.

"The lady said she wants to move on," said Roland, and gave Ship a very convincing serious cop look.

Delphine sat watching, fascinated. Male posturing was always so interesting! Also interesting was the fact that Ship hadn't brought up last night. But that was okay; they could all pretend it hadn't happened. It wouldn't matter after tonight either way. She wondered though if Ship knew he and Mitzi had been made tailing her car into Montrose. If Ship really was that clueless, how had he ever managed to survive at the Falls? Nepotism went a long way, she supposed.

Delphine gave Franko her car keys and asked him to bring in the non-lethal fruit punch that she'd splurged on.

"You betcha," he said. He kissed his wife on the cheek and left the table.

"You've got a good one there, Marvis," said Delphine.

"I sure do," she said. "It took a lot of training though."

Roland's head swung in her direction and his brows rose.

"Don't look so surprised," Marvis told him. "It's probably happening to you at home, and you don't even know it. We are very stealthy." She winked at him, and both she and Delphine laughed.

Roland and Delphine put their heads together. "Just about everyone is here," she said quietly. She tilted her head toward the back of the room, where Sylvie and Gerard were putting fresh pastries from Cousin Roman's Bakery on the refreshments table. Tonight's food and drink selection were top-notch, thought Delphine. She made a note to talk to Franko after all this about making some permanent upgrades.

Sylvie caught Delphine's gaze and waved. Her blond hair was piled on her head in a loose updo, and the cut of her blue velvet dress revealed a trim figure that had withstood the many years of cheese taste-testing quite well. Sylvie elbowed Gerard, who looked at Delphine and held up a croissant. His figure had not withstood the many years of croissant tasting, but he still looked very handsome in his black suit. She hoped the croissant had chocolate in it and that he would save it for her.

Roland seemed to be staring at the front door, and when she followed his gaze, there stood Richard and Juliette.

"See that tall, dark-haired woman with the low-cut dress?" Delphine asked him.

"She's kind of hard to miss," said Roland.

"Yes, well, that's Richard's wife, Juliette."

"No," said Roland, sounding truly baffled. "Humpty's wife?"

She nodded. "Don't ask me how he does it."

"I don't want to ask you how he does it, I want to ask *him*," said Roland.

They watched as Juliette let out a laugh, hair bouncing around her tanned shoulders.

"Does she look like your wife?" Delphine asked Roland.

He blushed. "Um, no. My wife is … much more radiant."

By this time Franko was back at the table, seated next to

Marvis and holding a small paper bag filled with popcorn. "What did I miss?" he asked.

"Nothing yet," she said. "

"Thank goodness," he said, settling in with his snack. "This ought to be good."

Ship was also staring at Juliette. He adjusted the collar of his suit jacket and took a deep breath. "Time for the master to get to work," he said, and made to stand up.

"I don't think so," said Delphine, putting a hand on his arm. She looked at Marvis and nodded. Marvis' jaw clenched in concentration, and she bounced once in her chair.

A split-second later, Ship yelped. "Ow!"

"If you value your other shin, you'll stay put," said Marvis. "God, I've been wanting to do that for years."

Roland ran his fingers through his hair. "That's right, sporto, time for the real master to step in." He gave Ship a crooked smile and eased his way across the room.

Delphine watched as Roland got into position behind Juliette and Richard. As soon as he was stationary, Mitzi Bouffant appeared at his side. She said something to him, and he leaned down to listen. Then he shook his head and smiled politely. Mitzi latched onto his arm and began to lean all her weight forward. It looked like she was trying to pull him onto the dance floor. He shook his head again and tried to pry her fingers from his arm.

Delphine worried that she might have to send someone over there to rescue Roland from Mitzi's clutches. The poor man— fifteen years on the force, only to be taken down by one Pasadena senior citizen. Mitzi pulled and pulled, and Delphine feared that if the woman's hands accidentally slipped from Roland's arm, she would go flying across the room.

Roland leaned down and said something else to her. Her hands flew from his arm, and she looked at him with such indignation that Delphine smiled. Mitzi hit Roland with her handbag and stormed off, and Delphine laughed.

# CHAPTER 25

"Okay then," said Delphine, and Marvis stood up and left the table.

"Okay what?" Ship reached under the table to rub his shin again.

"Okay, hello there," said Sylvie, sitting down in the chair Marvis had just vacated. She looked even more stunning up close, and as predicted, Ship couldn't take his eyes off her.

Delphine silently blessed the woman for agreeing to help with the plan—and being so good at providing a distraction.

Marvis had made her way to the back of the room and stood next to Gerard DeDieu, who was eating a Ritz cracker with spray cheese. There was no accounting for taste, Delphine reminded herself. Marvis pretended to reach for a cracker right as Gerard went for another one. They bumped hands, she laughed, and Delphine watched as they began to chat. Trap set.

Until everything could get sorted, almost everyone in attendance was a suspect, and needed to be treated with caution. It was challenging to keep her attention on multiple places at once, but not impossible.

"Thank you for your service," Delphine said to Franko, the

wonderfully patient husband, who was still sitting at the table and also had his eye on his wife.

"The things we do for our country," he said. He stood up, saluted Delphine, and walked into the crowd.

The first song of the evening started to play, and it was time for Delphine to get into position too. She glanced at Ship and Sylvie, huddled together in conversation. He'd forgotten about dancing with Delphine. Perfect.

Sylvie got up and pulled at Shipley's sleeve. They made their way onto the floor and began to dance. She was better than Delphine expected, considering Gerard had said she wasn't very good. Maybe most people weren't good, compared to Gerard. In any case, perhaps she'd invite Sylvie to join the Trotting Foxes when this was all over, as well as Judy. They would probably all get along well as friends, if they made it through the night.

Delphine eyed Judy and Frances, who were the last two still sitting at the table. "Will you two be all right here?" she asked.

Frances took the liberty of answering for both of them. "Oh sure! Me and my new pal will lay low and watch all the hot guys."

"We'll be fine," said Judy, not sounding very convinced.

Delphine made her way to the front of the room and from there skirted the growing crowd until she stood next to Richard. She thought it wouldn't take him long to notice her standing there, what with him being the top regional agent of an elite international spy organization. But no. Nothing. Time for her to nudge things in the right direction.

She looked at Roland, who stood near Juliette. Go time.

Delphine tapped Richard on the elbow, while Roland walked to stand right in front of Juliette. As he began to engage her in conversation, Delphine tapped Richard again, who noticed her that time.

The first song ended and the second began to play.

"Let's dance," suggested Delphine. She tried to keep her face clear of any emotion. When he didn't move, she gave him a fake smile tugged on his sleeve. For a moment she worried she might have to pull a Mitzi and muscle him out onto the parquet floor, but he relented and they walked into the crowd.

Roland had already led Juliette out to the dance floor, and they were attempting some sort of activity that was supposed to be dancing. Richard was also watching them.

"They make a nice couple, don't they?" asked Delphine. Richard glowered at her as they embraced and began their own pathetic attempt at a foxtrot.

"I'm surprised you had the courage to show up here tonight," said Richard.

"Why wouldn't I?"

"I could question you for additional questions. I mean, I could take you in right now."

"Oh, you won't do that," she said. "That would end badly for you. However, this evening will end badly for you either way."

"What's that supposed to mean?"

Sylvie and Ship glided by, and Delphine watched Richard's reaction to seeing their former informant. Genuine surprise.

"Another old friend is here too," Delphine said, and turned her gaze to the back of the room. Marvis had successfully kept Gerard anchored to the snack table. "We are all here to see you and Ship fall. Well, everyone except Simon."

"What?" he asked, losing step with her. Not that they'd ever been in step, thanks to Richard's leg. He always landed more heavily on his shorter leg and instead of their movements feeling like a smooth flow of actions, the dance felt more like the herky-jerky movement of a roller coaster being pulled by a squeaky chain up to the top of a giant rise. *Look out, Richard,* thought Delphine. *Here comes the drop.*

"You framed me with that Beaufort," Delphine said. "You set me up. I'm no more the Big Cheese than she is." She pointed to Juliette, looking very comfortable in the arms of Roland

Magnusson—who also looked a little too comfortable, in Delphine's opinion. But she crossed her fingers that he'd be ready to spring into action when he was needed, for the sake of the mission's success.

"Bastard!" shouted a woman from across the dance floor. A few people stopped dancing, and Delphine and Richard watched Sylvie slap Shipley's face as the two of them stood in the middle of the room. That was the sign that Sylvie had gotten the information she was after. They'd been right—Ship had been in on framing Delphine as the Big Cheese. Of course he had. Now it was time to find out more.

"You had some help, naturally," Delphine said to Richard as they started dancing again.

"I don't know what you're talking about," he said. "The fingerprints on the cheese were conclusively yours."

"Way back when, you tried to frame Sylvie," she went on. "She told us all about it. She made the mistake of trusting you to hold up your end of a very unsavory bargain, but instead you blackmailed her into obscurity and conveniently inferred she was the smuggler. Why would you do that? So you could take everything over. And you've been running things ever since. Now, for some reason the heat's been turned up and you need yet another scapegoat. This time it's me."

He was silent as they passed by Juliette and Roland again. They had never moved from their starting point, both of them being too two-left-footed to make much progress.

"Did you ever stop to think that perhaps Sylvie has been lying to you?" asked Richard. "Ask yourself what she could lose if you knew the tooth. I mean truth."

Delphine's mind raced. "Are you and she—?"

Richard laughed. "Oh please," he said. "Look at her. And then look at Juliette."

"True. You always did like them young and not very smart."

"Oh Delphine, you only see what you thought you saw. I

mean, you saw what ... You don't know what you're talking about."

The song would end soon. Delphine mentally shuffled through the next steps of her plan. She realized she had to be more careful than she'd originally thought—she might not be the only one in the room who was planning a confrontation tonight.

"Come with me," she said, pointing to the back of the studio.

Richard tried to stand his ground. "Why should I?"

"Because if you don't, I'll break your legs before you can say Beaufort d'Alpage."

Delphine was tense but excited; she was on the verge of finally being able to use her strong-arm tactics against someone, and the prospect made her happier than it should have. Roland caught her eye with a questioning glance, and she shook her head. He was to stay in position and keep dancing with Juliette.

Sylvie guided Ship, who was still shell-shocked from the slap, to the back of the studio as well. Delphine and Richard had been dancing near the front of the room and were close on their heels. The four of them walked down the dark hallway and out the emergency exit. They came out into the alley behind the strip mall. Marvis and Gerard joined them a few seconds later. The alley was deserted, save for a raccoon digging through a trash can ten yards away.

The group was well-matched. Delphine was the most fit of everyone, and Sylvie had confessed she also had some fighting skills. Jiujitsu, if Delphine wasn't mistaken. Shipley and Richard were trained, but Richard was dreadfully out of shape and Ship had never been a match for her. This wasn't Marvis' fight, and she'd never been in the Falls, but as Delphine's dear friend, she knew what was at stake and could give someone a good kick to the shins—or a little higher up, if need be. They stood in a loose circle and eyed each other with suspicion.

"Let's get to the bottom of this right now," demanded Delphine. "Richard, you and Shipley had someone put those wheels of Beafuort in my car and then faked the report stating my prints were on them. You were so obvious, it was pathetic. One of you has been the Big Cheese ever since you killed Simon and took over from him."

"I told you, Sylvie was le Grande Fromage," said Richard.

Gerard's mouth dropped open and he stared at Sylvie. "Non!"

"No," said Delphine. "Sylvie was not the Big Cheese. Simon was. She was going to take it over after his retirement, but he died and then either you or Ship moved in and beat her to it."

"Sylvie, is this true?" asked Gerard. "You did all this with the cheese?"

Sylvie rolled her eyes. "Honestly, Gerard, you are about as smart as a round of Brie."

"But I never knew!" he exclaimed. "Was it you who did the laundering of the money?"

"She said she wasn't the Big Cheese," said Delphine, trying but failing to be patient.

"The money came from Simon, Gerard. Mon dieu," said Sylvie.

"That's mon *deDieu*!" said Ship. He looked from face to face expectantly, waiting for a laugh. "Or is that mon fondue? Haha…"

Sylvie shook her head and pinched the bridge of her nose.

"You are incorrect as usual," Richard said to Delphine.

"Really," said Delphine. She looked at Shipley.

Shipley cocked his hip and said, "Well, *I* don't know about any Big Cheese thing. But I can tell you what happened to Simon."

Richard stared at him. "What are you talking about?" He sounded like he was trying to speak to a fourth grader.

Ship put a hand out to silence him. "I'm tired of lying about it. It's time the truth came out. I can't hold it in any longer."

He was being so dramatic that Delphine almost expected him to swoon. Her pulse raced in anticipation. The answer, finally!

Marvis's eyes moved from person to person as they spoke, a bright smile on her face. She seemed to be enjoying the volley of information even though she knew nothing about the case.

"We were at the Cheese Store of Beverley Hills—me, Simon,

and Delphine," said Ship. "I remember it was pretty hot that day, and we learned about how cheese weeps. It was so sad, haha!"

"Don't do this," snapped Richard.

"Simon said he didn't feel very well and needed to go outside. Instead of heading out front, he went out the back. I think he wanted to have a cigarette but didn't want anyone to know he smoked."

"Everyone knew he smoked," said Delphine.

Sylvie said, "The vanity of men."

"Pffft!" said Richard.

"Oh that's funny, coming from you," snapped Delphine, and Sylvie laughed.

"Anyway," said Ship, clearly disappointed that the focus had shifted away from his story, "a few minutes later I went out to check on him and there he was, being held up by a mugger! In Beverley Hills, of all places. Crazy." Ship stopped and closed his eyes, letting out a dramatic sigh. "Okay, this is so hard..." His voice had a quiver to it, as if he were trying not to cry. Delphine was perplexed and intrigued.

"The mugger hadn't seen me because I was behind him. He was a pretty small guy, and I thought I could sneak up and disarm him, but it didn't work. We struggled, and well, the gun went off." Ship wiped a tear from his eye. "The mugger ran away, with his weapon, I might add, and I went back inside as soon as I could compose myself. You know the rest."

"So you shot Simon Pegbottam," said Delphine.

"Maybe," said Ship. "But I'm pretty sure it was the other guy. In any case I feel terrible about it."

"The investigation was inconclusive," said Richard. "It's in the past. We should let it go."

Sylvie lunged at Ship with a raised fist. "Morceau de merde!" she shrieked.

Gerard managed to hook her arm right before she reached her intended target and pulled her back. "Not worth your trouble, mon cheri," he said.

"It was inconclusive because you either didn't investigate or covered up your findings," said Delphine, thinking out loud.

Her mind raced as she tried to process what she'd learned so far. Simon's death had been an accident? She hadn't noticed Simon slipping out the back of the cheese store and also hadn't noticed Ship's absence. She'd been focused on learning about cheese, sure, but was that an excuse for being so ignorant? Suddenly she began to doubt herself. What else had she not noticed over the course of her career? All that would have to wait; now was the time to connect the past to the present once and for all.

By this point, the raccoon had stopped rummaging in the trash can, and Delphine kept an eye on it as it crept toward them. It stopped about five yards behind Richard and watched them all argue. She was kind of disappointed it didn't come any closer. It might have been fun to watch her old boss get attacked by a crazy rabid animal.

Think, Delphine, think! It was possible that Ship was the Big Cheese—it *had* to be him or Richard. Time to go with signs from the universe. The racoon was clearly watching Richard now. She silently thanked the animal.

"Richard took over as Big Cheese regardless," she said, gesturing with her hands. She looked at him. "You ran it for years, with no one suspecting anything."

"Hmph," said Sylvie, who followed her declaration of disdain with a few French curse words.

"Until recently," Delphine continued. "Richard, you got greedy. You knew the Falls wanted you to retire, but you still needed money for your new hobby."

"You've got a new hobby?" asked Ship. "What is it? Are you taking golf lessons?"

"His hobby is his new wife, you ass," said Marvis.

"You needed a way to launder money faster. That's why you were looking into buying the Sassy Steppers," said Delphine. "But somewhere along the way, you screwed up. You were under pressure, and you got sloppy."

Everyone was silent and all eyes were on Richard. He moved his hand to reach inside his jacket, and Delphine's senses went on high alert. She prayed that her mic was recording everything, and she regretted not having pulled her .38 from her ankle holster before this all started. She must've been so anxious about the confrontation that she'd forgotten. Another strike against her...

She put one foot slightly in front of the other, ready to pounce on him if he pulled a weapon from his coat pocket. Ship stood between her and Richard, and she would possibly have to take him out too, on her way to get to her old boss. This wouldn't be easy, but she'd give it her best shot, and hope that Sylvie and Marvis would catch on fast enough to come to her aid. She held her breath...

But Richard didn't pull a gun. Instead, he brought out a package of gum and took a stick before offering the pack to the group.

"Oh yes, please!" said Ship. "You never know when your life might depend on fresh breath. Haha..."

Delphine clenched her jaw. If she ended up not being able to pin any of this on Shipley, by god she would make sure he got fired for being completely clueless.

"Your deductive skills are as sharp ever, Delphine," said Richard. "And as usual, you're not quite sup to peed."

"What did he say?" Gerard asked Sylvie.

Delphine was on the verge of putting a hand under her chin so that her jaw wouldn't drop to the ground with surprise. Everyone looked confused.

"That's right," Richard said. "I never got the chance to be the Big Cheese. Someone else took over before I could figure out how to do it myself."

"But you blackmailed Sylvie to get rid of her," said Delphine. "She was out of the picture."

"Yes, and it would have worked great if I hadn't been too late."

Ship put a hand to his chest. "Me? Has it been me this whole time?" Someone threw the pack of gum at him.

In a flash, Delphine knew. She turned to Sylvie. "We've got to—"

But she never finished the sentence. Delphine's world went dark.

# CHAPTER 26

Roland started to get worried when, by the end of the third song of the evening, Delphine hadn't returned from the alley behind the dance studio. Also, his toes were starting to hurt from being stepped on so often by his dance partner, Juliette Dere.

Now that he was up close to her, Roland realized she was older than he'd first thought. She was still stunning though. Maybe she used a lot of expensive face products or something. All women did that, right? Roland knew his own wife had a separate budget for beauty stuff and he wagered Juliette's budget was quite a bit more. No offense to Christina, he thought. Then he felt guilty.

But he had a job to do. So he smiled at Juliette, and she gave him a polite smile back. Perhaps she was in her mid- to late-fifties, he figured. Still, that was younger than anyone he'd been hanging out with since he'd gotten to LA, save for little Zooey. Juliette's relatively youthful demeanor was downright refreshing in comparison to his companions for the previous night's tiki bar escapade.

"How long did you say you've been dancing?" he asked her. The music had stopped for a moment, but Roland's assignment was to keep her on the dance floor, so he'd have to rely on his charm and conversational skills.

"Not that long," she said in her French accent. It wasn't as strong as Sylvie's, but it was pronounced enough to be recognizable, and European enough to be alluring. "I saw a show on the TV about dancing—you know *Dancing with the Stars*? So much fun. Jennifer Grey was on one season. Do you remember her? She was in that movie *Dirty Dancing*. I love that movie. Such a shame about Patrick Swayze…"

"Uh-huh," said Roland, who tried to tune out her continuous chatter again. She stepped on his foot. Even without music she was a menace.

Delphine had told Roland all about her former boss Richard, and what a pompous misogynist he was. And after Sylvie had told them what he'd done to her, it was a pleasure to steal the man's wife away for a few dances. Sometimes Roland loved his job—to dance with a beautiful woman wasn't much of an imposition, except he wasn't sure his feet would ever recover from the sharp heels of her shoes. Even to his untrained eye, her footwear did not look like they were made for dancing.

The music started up again, this time a lively vintage swing number. He'd been hoping for another slower song, like the previous Tommy Dorsey and Frank Sinatra tune. Slower songs meant slower footwork, and that could result in fewer foot injuries. But no such luck.

They began dancing, not going quite as quickly as the other experienced dancers, but still managing to move around the room a little.

"This is a lot of fun," said Roland. "I love this song."

"This is not like the music in *Dirty Dancing*. I have that record at home and it's—"

A distant *pop!* echoed through the studio just as the song ended. It had sounded a lot like a gunshot.

Juliette leaned in close to Roland, stopping only when her lips brushed his ear. "Your friend won't be coming back in," she whispered in her sensuous French accent.

At first, Roland had found the accent charming. But after getting his toes turned into hamburger meat by her insidious high heels and listening to her blab on about absolutely nothing all night, he'd started to wonder if perhaps her voice was in fact a harbinger of doom. Now he knew it was. And come to think of it, something about her perfume reminded him of ... smoked Gouda?

"You're the Big Cheese," he said in a whisper.

He tried to push himself away, but she pulled him closer with a surprising amount of force, and the lapels of his suit jacket collided violently with her decolletage. Their eyes locked and her gaze was intense, but unreadable, and for several seconds, Roland was very confused. Until she spoke again. "You're not going anywhere, Detective."

When she released her grip on his coat, she held his gun in her hand, and it was pointed at the left side of his ribcage. Delphine was going to give him the worst time about this if he didn't think of something heroic, and fast.

"But how? Why?" he asked. Not much had come to mind yet that resembled a plan.

"I have been the Big Cheese ever since Simon Pegbottam was killed, god rest his soul." She looked downright rueful, as if she were remembering something sad. "He was my father, you see."

Roland laughed. "No way! What, were you twelve when you took over his operation?"

She smiled at him; an awfully disarming, warm smile for someone still aiming a gun at him. "You're sweet, but no."

"Oh, so you've had some work done." Roland watched her elegant eyebrows furrow. "I mean, you take great care of yourself!"

Now she looked angry, and Roland feared she might accidentally—or on purpose—squeeze the trigger. To be shot with his own service weapon ... He'd never live it down.

"And, uh, was your mom French?" he tried.

"That is a brilliant deduction."

Roland tried to think of more ways to stall. "Wow."

She looked at him as if disappointed that was all he could come up with. He was disappointed too.

"Did your dad train you? I thought he was training someone else."

Her expression turned hard. "He involved me in the family business but said he would not let me take over. Too risky for his 'little girl,' he said. Well, the title is rightfully mine. And it has been, ever since my father's unfortunate death. I earned it, and cheese has been very good to me."

"Then what happened to draw you out after all these years?" he asked.

"That blasted Richard!"

"Okay," said Roland, almost—but not quite—forgetting there was a gun jabbed in his ribs at this point. "I just gotta know. Why on earth did you marry that guy?"

She rolled her eyes and looked like maybe she'd forgotten she was jabbing a gun into his ribs. "That was meant as a strategic move. After the recession, margins got thin and I had to take more risks. His organization could provide me cover as I expanded my business. I admit, not my best idea. He always means well, but he is weak. He told me he could handle more responsibility, but he wasn't doing enough."

Roland shook his head and *tsked* her. "You got greedy," he said.

"Look at me."

Roland kept looking at the gun in her hand.

"I said, *look* at me," she hissed.

His eyes trailed from the gun up her bare arm to her tanned shoulder, then made a brief stop at her cleavage before moving on to take in her collagen-filled lips, and coming to rest on her face.

"Looking like this has a high price. Richard doesn't

understand the economics of beauty. To be honest, I can see why all five of his marriages, including this one, have failed."

Roland wondered if one of the problems in his own marriage was that he, too, didn't understand the economics of beauty. What man did? But surely not all women played these games. However, maybe he should consider taking his wife to a day spa after all. If he managed to survive his night of ballroom dancing.

Roland looked deeper into her eyes and saw more sadness and regret than anger. "You're so beautiful," he said. He reached out to tuck a lock of hair behind her ear … and went for the gun with his other hand.

But he'd underestimated her strength and her focus, and instead of taking control of his weapon, he got a smack on the wrist with it and then a hard jab in the ribs.

"That mistake will cost you," she said. Her eyes flicked to the back of the room and then to his face. "Let's get going, Roland. Your attempts to outsmart le Grande Fromage are coming to their conclusion." She jerked her head at the front entrance and indicated he should lead the way.

He couldn't leave Delphine in the alley! She might be bleeding to death that very minute. But there was nothing he could do from inside the studio, not with his own gun pointed at his back.

"One more thing," said Roland over his shoulder. "Why Delphine?"

"Oh, that. There has been weakness in my supply chain. As I tried to expand, we had to make more connections. Richard said he could take care of it, but he screwed up. Someone was onto us and I told him to fix it, so he chose Delphine to take the fall. He never liked her, said she had a bad attitude and that this would be the perfect payback. But that, too, he ruined. And here we are. Honestly, he will have to go. Right after you and your partner, of course."

"How ironic," Roland said. "Humpty Dumpty takes a big fall."

"What?" said Juliette from behind him.

He stopped and turned around—she'd be crazy to shoot him in here.

"Nothing. Wouldn't it have been easier for you to go after Sylvie? I mean, it would have been a lot easier to imagine her as the Big C instead of Delphine."

A torrent of French curse words, or what he assumed were curse words, came from Juliette's mouth, and he smiled. Sometimes people took the long way around an otherwise short path, and that was fine with him, because in his experience, that was how criminals ended up getting caught. Now he just had to figure out how to get out of being caught himself, so he could do some catching.

"Get moving," she said at the end of her tirade, and motioned for the door again.

They had almost made it out when Roland spotted Kenji and Frances through the huge floor-to-ceiling windows. They stood outside chatting in the harsh glare of a bank of overhead fluorescent lights; the same kind that seemed to illuminate every strip mall sidewalk across the country. Frances' purse dangled off one arm and Kenji held a cigarette. Who still smoked these days?

As Roland opened the studio door, Kenji made eye contact but showed no sign of taking any action. Roland felt an inkling of panic and tried to push the feeling down. He had to keep his head, not only for his own sake, but for that of Delphine. Who knew what had happened around back. Surely if Kenji and Frances had realized something happened to their friend, they'd be headed for the alley instead of jibber-jabbering out front. If only he could let them know somehow. He could handle Juliette himself. Most likely.

# CHAPTER 27

Delphine couldn't see a thing with Richard's arm across her face. He must have been trying to hit her in the head, but since she'd already turned to leave, he missed and all she got was a face full of Italian-suit sleeve. She pulled away enough to be able to see again, and that was when he came at her with full force, arms outstretched and a maniacal look on his face.

But Richard was so out of fighting shape that he came across more like a flailing Muppet than a trained assassin. Delphine planted her feet for the attack and Sylvie appeared at her side. Together they fended him off, and Delphine went for one of his arms while Sylvie went for the other.

Delphine secured Richard's left arm with ease. Piece of cake! But a split-second later, she realized her celebration was premature.

"Delphine!" cried Sylvie. "I can't—"

Richard had evaded Sylvie's grasp on his right arm. She'd given it her best try, but she hadn't been trained for this type of maneuvering like Delphine had. Plus, Richard was right-handed, and that side of his upper body was probably stronger. In retrospect the two women should have switched sides, but there'd been no time to instruct Sylvie in nuances like that. It was just like dancing. You and your partner had to be of the same mind, whether you wanted to win a foxtrot trophy or come out on top in a scrappy back-alley brawl.

Delphine watched as Richard continued to elude Sylvie's grasp and reached into his inside coat pocket again, this time bringing forth a pistol.

She lunged for the weapon, but it only caused him to fling his arm around wildly, risking harm to everyone in the group. He grunted as Delphine grabbed for his hand and in the scuffle, the gun went off.

The bullet hit Richard's left foot. "I'm hit! I'm hit! Ow, watch it!" he barked.

Delphine plucked the gun from his hand and gave it to Sylvie. "Relax, chief. The bullet barely grazed your shoe." She secured Richard's hands behind his back with a zip tie she produced from her cleavage.

When she looked up from her task, she noticed Gerard and Sylvie were captivated by a different scene. She followed their line of sight just in time to see the racoon, who apparently couldn't resist getting in on the action, creep closer and nip Shipley in the ankle.

He lost his balance and rolled around on the ground, clutching his foot. Delphine swore she saw the racoon give the man a satisfied nod before scampering down the alley.

Marvis began laughing and couldn't seem to stop, but being the good-natured woman Delphine knew her to be, she walked to Shipley and extended a hand to help him up. He looked up at Marvis like she was a hostile alien creature, and must have mistaken her assistance for aggression, because he began clawing at her and shrieking like a little girl. A well-timed kick to the family jewels by Marvis took him down again, and that time he stayed down long enough for Delphine to hand Richard off to Gerard and take care of securing Shipley.

When the two men stood side-by-side, hands bound behind their backs, Delphine took Richard's pistol from Sylvie and trained it on her two former colleagues.

"Now the truth will come out. About everything from the past, and how it all connects to your attempt to frame me," she said.

# CHAPTER 28

Delphine waited in the shadows behind a column outside the dance studio's front door. She'd handed Richard's gun back over to Sylvie and instructed her and the group to keep the two criminals locked in the dance studio's office until she could take care of the real Big Cheese and call in the authorities.

She had a slight headache, and something didn't feel quite right in her left elbow; when she rubbed the tendons in her forearm, they were tender. Too much topspin on her forehand back in the nineties, when she'd attempted (successfully, of course) to penetrate a ring of tennis-playing art forgers in Monaco. The struggle in the alley a few minutes prior had caused a flare-up. These days, some things didn't heal up as well as they used to, and other things seemed to stop working from time to time. Unfortunate.

She peered around the edge of the column just as Roland come to an abrupt stop near Frances and Kenji. Juliette had been following Roland so closely that she almost knocked him over when he stopped moving.

Roland wore a look of desperation as he caught Kenji's eye. But Kenji, and even Frances, kept their cool. Delphine was so proud. Her body tensed and she gripped her pistol, ready to make her move.

It was then that Kenji's eyes flicked to hers, as did Frances'. Delphine gave them the tiniest of nods. Kenji's unlit cigarette dangled from the side of his mouth, and he stepped back to lean against the front windows of the ScriptDoctor storefront, hands in pockets. His gaze moved back to Roland, who, bless him, caught on that something was about to happen.

Frances pulled her purse off her arm and gripped the handles with a white-knuckled hand.

Delphine stepped around the stuccoed column. "Hello, Juliette dear."

Both Juliette and Roland whipped around to see Delphine standing there smiling.

It was only then that Delphine realized Juliette was holding a gun, and she knew this because it was now pointed right at her. Delphine had missed it. How could she have forgotten to consider the possibility that Juliette was armed? It looked like she was about to pay for her mistake.

Delphine walked forward and raised her own pistol. She would not doubt herself in this moment; she had not lost her touch. This was a dance of sorts, and she knew the steps.

Almost in slow motion, she registered the look on Juliette's face and seemed to feel rather than see the woman's body go rigid. Delphine continued to breathe, slow and steady, gun held lightly in her hand. It was as if her feet floated above the sidewalk —like floating along a dance floor. Her senses were heightened, and she was attuned to her partner. Or in this case, her enemy. Perhaps sometimes they were the same thing?

Then Delphine prepared to hone her aim and fire. But when she tried to flex her arm … nothing happened. The muscles around her right elbow had frozen! What a time to get a case of tennis elbow. She tried again but still couldn't steady the gun. Milliseconds felt like years. Her stomach dropped in abject fear, and so many thoughts rushed through her head so quickly that they congealed into a ball of confusion.

For some reason the next thought she had was, *When did Kenji start smoking?*

What occurred next took a very short period of time, but Delphine's senses were so heightened from adrenaline that it felt like they went on for ages.

Roland turned to Juliette and must have figured out he was in less danger than Delphine, and he attempted to grab her. But before he could manage it, Frances stepped away from the wall and brought her purse down on Juliette's arm from behind so hard that the gun fell from her hand and skittered off the sidewalk, coming to rest under a late-model Cadillac.

"Hot dang!" said Frances. "Bullseye. Take that, you hussy!"

Juliette turned toward her attacker, but instead of hitting Frances, she only managed to get as far as punching Roland in the face. His hands flew to his nose as his eyes went wide, and he let loose with a monologue of very inventive cusswords.

This bought Delphine a few seconds, but she still had to figure out another way to take down Juliette, since using her gun was out of the question. And she needed to do it now; no time to second-guess herself. But the diminishment of her skills as a deadly agent was undeniable, and the specter of her aging body also raised its head, bringing on a case of existential dread so terrifying that she felt paralyzed.

Before Delphine could regain her composure, Kenji went into action. The man pushed away from the wall so quickly he was a blur as he removed the unlit cigarette from his mouth and headed straight for his target. Once in striking distance, he snapped the cigarette in two and blew the shreds of tobacco right at Juliette's face.

Her countenance transformed into a frightening grimace. "Aaahhh! Aaahhh-*choo!*"

Juliette let out a sneeze so powerful it could've counted as a mild flare-up of LA's famous Santa Ana winds. Her long hair flew everywhere as she doubled over.

By then, Roland had recovered from his bop on the nose, which was intact and bloodless, thank goodness. A fiendishly malicious smile overcame his face, and he stomped his right Doc Marten down hard on Juliette's left foot.

"Payback!" he shouted.

"Merde!" said Juliette. She kicked off her heels faster than Delphine thought possible, considering they had been strapped to the woman's feet and ankles. But off they came, and Juliette shot across the walkway and made for the parking lot at an awkward, yet speedy, gait.

This was where Delphine had her opponent beat. Her elbow might have been out of commission, but her legs and feet were not. She caught up with Juliette before Roland was even halfway across the sidewalk.

"You get 'er, D!" yelled Frances.

And get 'er Delphine did. She tripped Juliette, who went sprawling into the Cadillac. Roland peeled her off the hood and held her arms behind her back.

"Get off me, you stupid American policeman!" screeched Juliette.

"Oh, that really hurts," said Roland, holding her with ease even though she struggled to free herself. The woman might have been a cheese kingpin (queenpin?), but athleticism was not one of her strong suits.

"I thought you didn't want to be part of this," said Roland, glaring at Kenji.

Kenji shrugged. "I wanted to see how it ended."

"Are you okay?" Roland scrutinized Delphine for signs of injury. "I thought you might have gotten shot out back."

"Oh no, not me, dear. But I'm afraid Richard's dancing days are over."

Juliette struggled against Roland's grip, but to no avail. She was no longer a threat and something inside Delphine relaxed a tiny bit.

"Where's Judy?" she asked.

"A very hot guy came up to our table and asked her to dance," said Frances. "If she's smart, she's still in there giving him her best moves."

Delphine knew Judy would have wanted to see her boss and his wife get taken down, but she understood. Sometimes romance came first. Maybe that was something she should try to prioritize more often too.

Juliette spoke rapid-fire French at no one in particular.

"This one's got a potty mouth!" said Frances, pointing a thumb at Roland's prisoner. "You should be careful what you say, honey. Some of us here know French and you wouldn't want to incriminate yourself further."

"What are you, some kind of attorney?" snapped Juliette.

"Yes," said Frances. "But not for people like you."

Delphine noticed a few people standing nearby in front of the improv studio. "Let's take this someplace else. We're drawing a crowd."

Juliette gave Delphine a poisonous look. "You think you have solved all your problems," she gasped, "but I assure you, they are just beginning!"

Still silent, Kenji handed Delphine a nylon zip tie, and she expertly bound Juliette's hands behind her back.

"No, I don't think so," said Delphine. "I'm out of the cheese game. However, a nice grilled Gruyere sandwich sounds pretty good right about now. What do you say, boys?"

# CHAPTER 29

Shortly after capturing the infamous Big Cheese, Roland watched with pride as Delphine handed Juliette, Richard, and Shipley over to Charles Bing, the director of the Fall's Western States division, and his team for processing and disciplinary action. For now, Charles had accepted Delphine and Roland's word as enough to hold the three miscreants, but Delphine would still have to write up a full report and present Charles' team with their recorded evidence.

The next order of business was recovering Roland's gun from under the Cadillac sedan, which was harder than expected because the only person flexible enough to attempt it was busy debriefing her superiors. An argument ensued between Roland, Frances, and Kenji about how to best go about the task. Kenji insisted he didn't want to help, but when Roland pointed out he'd already broken his "I'm not getting my hands dirty" rule, Kenji acquiesced and crawled underneath the vehicle to retrieve it. So far, Delphine was still unaware that the gun Juliette had been holding was his, and hopefully it wouldn't come back to bite him later.

Now Roland, Delphine, Kenji, Sylvie, and Gerard sat at a table in a hole-in-the-wall dive called the Cheese Cellar. Located in

Glendale, it was, as the name implied, dark and cave-like. Dim lighting cast by several wall sconces and an elaborate chandelier threw shadows on the bare brick walls, and the scents of butter, cheese, and freshly baked bread wafted through the air. Roland wondered if his new suit would smell like grease in the morning, but he didn't care—the food was so good.

After everyone enjoyed a selection of fruits and nuts and drank shots of cherry brandy (in keeping with the Swiss belief that the liquor helped to digest cheese), the main meal was served and they sat in reverent silence, looking at the beautiful spread before them: the fanciest artisanal grilled cheese sandwiches ever invented, accompanied by a light side-salad and a dry white wine —also a Swiss tradition. Roland had insisted on taking photos of the plates and right before they dug in, Delphine raised her wineglass and proposed a toast.

"To Simon," she said.

Everyone stayed silent for a beat before answering. "To Simon," they said.

Each sandwich was a masterpiece of the most delicate flavors and freshest ingredients, and there was no conversation for the first few minutes as they ate with concentration.

"This place is like a magical kingdom," said Kenji. He sat at the head of the table with his eyes closed and head bowed as he took another bite. They were about halfway through the meal and starting to slow their pace.

"I wonder if Miami has places like this," said Roland.

"No," said Sylvie. "They have a few cheese shops, but Los Angeles is the epicenter of the cheese underground. If you are a connoisseur, this is the place to be."

Roland leaned toward Delphine. "Another point in LA's favor."

"Yes," said Delphine. "If you are ranking places to live, I'm sure easy access to rare cheese is a significant factor."

"It is for some of us!" said Gerard, looking offended.

Near the end of the meal, Gerard ordered them some hot tea

and Delphine launched into the story of what happened behind the dance studio to catch Roland up to speed, but mostly because Kenji kept asking about it every ten minutes.

She told them about the discussion in the alley, including Shipley's story of what had happened to Simon Pegbottam all those years ago. She described accusing Richard of being the Big Cheese and then realizing she had been wrong. The part about the fighting had elicited color commentary from Gerard and Sylvie, much to the delight of everyone at the table, except maybe Delphine.

Roland shook his head in amazement. "What a story. I'm just glad no one else got hurt."

"Oh, but it gets better," said Delphine.

"Really?" asked Sylvie.

"Yes. After I took them all to Charles Bing and his team, Shipley found religion and unburdened himself of a few more very interesting facts."

"I bet Richard loved that," said Roland.

"Juliette did too," said Delphine.

Roland laughed. He could just picture Richard turning a bright shade of purple and Juliette hurling French curse words as Shipley went into confession mode.

"So what is the big news?" asked Sylvie.

"Juliette is Simon's daughter," she said.

"That part we know," said Sylvie. "Roland told us."

"Right, but apparently, the robber in the alley at the Beverley Hills cheese shop was Juliette!" Delphine said, raising both hands in excitement.

"No!" said Kenji.

"Yes," Delphine said. "She'd been trying to scare her father into handing over the business, to keep it in the family. Then Shipley showed up, thought she was a mugger, and in the scuffle, Simon … He…" Delphine struggled with the words.

"Juliette?" asked Roland. He still had trouble believing all of it.

Everyone at the table nodded but stayed quiet, as if deep in thought.

After a moment, Sylvie said, "I knew he had a daughter, and that she was familiar with the business, but he never said one word about her being interested in taking over."

Delphine nodded. "I guess it was the perfect setup for her since no one suspected her."

At that moment, Kenji let out a fantastic burp. "Excuse me," he said, dabbing his mouth with his cloth napkin. "Cheese."

Sylvie poured him more hot tea. "Drink this. The warmth will help with your digestion."

"I wonder what their deal was," said Gerard, tapping his bottom lip.

"Whose deal?" asked Delphine.

"Richard and Juliette. What an unlikely pair!"

"Marriage of convenience," said Delphine. "He tried proposing right after Simon was killed. Well, actually, Juliette confessed that Richard tried to blackmail her into marriage. But she outsmarted him, got out of the deal, *and* kept the cheese business."

"Why did she agree to marry him all these years later?" asked Roland.

Delphine shrugged. "Times had changed. It got harder to turn a profit. And they each had something the other wanted."

"Cheese?" asked Gerard.

Delphine gave him an exasperated look, then explained. "She had wealth and power. He had access to important contacts worldwide." She took a drink of her tea.

"Did you ever find out what Shippy's involvement was?" Roland asked Delphine.

Sylvie barked out a laugh. "That's an easy one."

Roland looked at her, waiting for her to elaborate, but it was Delphine who explained.

"Ship could never resist a pretty face. Juliette knew he was putty in her hands and used that to her advantage. He ran a lot of errands for her, including keeping tabs on us."

Roland thought about it. Of course that was it. Juliette was quite beautiful. And even though she was a few decades older than him, he might have been persuaded to give her a hand with a few things too. Maybe that was also part of the economics of beauty that she'd told him about. Women were so confusing.

The server came to the table with another pot of tea and some cookies that looked very boring, until Roland bit into one and almost experienced a religious conversion. "What are these?" he asked.

"French palmiers," said Gerard, biting into one. "I sell them at my bakery. These are quite good, but mine are better."

Roland definitely needed Delphine to take him back to the bakery before he left town so he could get some pastries. She'd been stingy sharing the chocolate croissant she brought home after her meeting with Gerard.

Delphine leaned back in her chair. "This is all so delicious," she said.

Roland turned in her direction. She looked tired, and more frail than she did when he'd arrived. There was no doubt she was a strong, clever woman, but the stress of the whole ordeal had taken a toll. He felt a sudden wave of tenderness toward her, seeing her in a different light. Before, she'd been a demanding and forceful presence who seemed to have complete control over his professional life. Now she was a woman who was tired and perhaps going through a reckoning of sorts.

"So, Sylvie," said Delphine. "I was wondering if you and Gerard would like to join the Trotting Foxes. It might be fun to have you both in the group."

"Yes, I might consider that," said Sylvie, and Gerard nodded with enthusiasm.

"Will you still work at the UCC?" Roland asked Sylvie.

She looked at him. "Why would you ask me that?"

"Because I might want to know where to find you if I decide to ask you out on another date," he said.

Gerard frowned. "Sylvie, you went on a date with this man?"

She gave him a kiss on the cheek. "Yes, but it meant nothing to me."

Roland put a hand on his heart. "Oh Sylvie, you're killing me over here. I can't believe our time together meant so little."

"Roland, darling. We had a nice evening, true. But you must let me go now. My heart belongs to another. You will get over me. In time."

Roland tried to look heartbroken and noticed Gerard had turned red. This was fun.

"Gerard, you and I never agreed to be exclusive," said Sylvie.

"Well, we are agreeing to it this very minute! Tu es ma petite amie!"

"You heard him, Roland," said Sylvie. Then she leaned across the table and whispered, "But you can come visit me anytime at the UCC."

"You're going to try to take over, aren't you?" he said, and everyone at the table stilled, except for Delphine, who looked unsurprised. She must have guessed it too.

Sylvie traced the top of her tea mug with her index finger and shrugged. "Nature abhors a vacuum, isn't that what they say?"

# CHAPTER 30

Delphine, Kenji, and Roland sat in the backyard with mugs of fresh tea, and their feet resting in some of Kenji's magic foot soak. That morning she'd slept in, allowing herself a bit more rest than usual, and even skipped yoga. Roland went without her. She hoped he would stick with it, as the flexibility one gained through the practice was invaluable. She wouldn't have made it through the last week if it weren't for her yoga. Of course, a little weight training and cardio also helped.

Roland was leaned back in his chair with sunglasses protecting his new shiner, courtesy of Juliette, from the warm California midmorning sun. "I could get used to life out here," he said.

"It is quite nice," said Delphine. "But we're in a quiet part of the city. And you also haven't had to go to the DMV or drive to Thousand Oaks at two in the afternoon."

"Like Miami is so great," he muttered.

"Hawaii is nice," said Kenji.

"Hmm." Delphine did love her home in Pasadena and enjoyed being close to her son Sean and his wife Zenia, and Zooey of course. She'd called Southern California home base for a long time, but perhaps she might be ready for a change of scenery, before it was too late to enjoy it.

"Hey, did you ever find Griffin a job?" asked Roland.

"Whatever made you think of that?" said Delphine.

"I don't know … Just wondering, I guess."

Delphine took his concern as a good sign. It was true, she had promised Griffin that she would help find her a new job. Delphine had been somewhat (okay, completely) responsible for Griffin being let go by the FBI. Delphine wasn't quite sure why she'd done it, only that she'd had a gut feeling that Griffin was unhappy in her forensics accounting job but would probably never do anything about it without a little push "from the universe," which in this case was her grandma. Plus, Griffin's husband Brian was a schmuck. She did owe it to Griffin to help the young woman find a new and interesting direction. She had a few ideas but kept getting … sidetracked.

"I am in the process of making some inquiries," she told Roland. "It's very nice of you to think of her."

"Yeah, well, she was nice, I guess," he said. A second later he sat upright. "There's one thing I don't get about this whole cheese thing though."

"Only one?" asked Kenji, who then laughed at his own joke. He sounded like a snake watching a sitcom. *Sss-sss-sss-sss.*

Roland glared at him for a moment before continuing. "Sylvie said she's going to take over as the Big Cheese. Yet you still invited her to join the Foxy Trots."

"That's the Trotting Foxes, dear," said Delphine.

"How did you become a detective?" asked Kenji. "You are terrible with names."

"That's what little pocket notebooks and smart phones are for, bro," said Roland. "And I happen to have many other valuable skills."

"Kenji, don't give him a hard time," said Delphine. "Roland is a very good detective."

"Hmph," said Kenji.

Delphine put down her tea. "If you recall, I asked her to join before she admitted her intentions. It would be impolite to rescind my invitation."

"Bull—poop," said Roland, pointing at her. "I don't buy it."

Of course he could read her. It was one of his many valuable skills. "Kenji," she said, "you were right the other day. About my motivations. It was fun to follow the mystery, there's no denying that. But I suppose part of me thought I could relive my younger days." She stopped to rub her elbow and looked at Roland as she continued. "Anyway, I'm officially retired, and whatever Sylvie chooses to do as a private citizen is her business. I'm done with it."

Delphine stared into the depths of her tea mug. "Charles Bing did ask me if I wanted to come back though."

"Wow!" said Roland. "That's cool."

Out of the corner of her eye, she saw Kenji turn in his chair to look at her. She knew what he was thinking. He probably missed the old days too, but that nostalgia came bundled with aching elbows and the innate sense that life was meant to slow down a bit when one reached their seventies. Not because they were too old to keep up, but because the wisdom that came with age dictated a desire for peace, rumination, perhaps even some solitude. To try to keep up with the young ones, or to continually pursue youth, was to miss the life that was right in front of you. Delphine didn't want to miss any of it.

"I don't want to go back to that life," she said. "I want a different one."

"What kind of life?" asked Kenji.

"I don't know," she said, and smiled at him. She knew that she wanted to always be friends with Kenji, but she also needed something more substantial. What that could be, she had no idea. Yet. "I guess I'll have to give that more thought."

"I was so afraid something bad happened to you in that alley," said Roland. "I heard the gunshot and…" His voice trailed off.

"That's sweet of you, dear," she said. "Is that why you looked so panic-stricken out front?"

"The fact that I had a gun jabbed into my back didn't help."

"That would do it," said Kenji.

"You could have helped out a little more," Roland said to Kenji. "You were right there."

Kenji furrowed his brow in consternation. "Yes, I was right there—with the sneezer."

"The what?" asked Roland.

"The cigarette trick. Old spy tactic. Over your head, kid." Kenji leaned back. "Besides, I knew Delphine would get everything under control. And remember, I didn't want to get involved."

Roland laughed. "That's rich."

"What do you mean?" asked Kenji.

"I think what he means is, you were awfully involved for someone who said they didn't want to be involved," said Delphine.

Kenji looked at his tea mug. "Oh. Well, it all worked out."

They splashed their feet around in the tepid water. Delphine's feet hadn't felt this good in years—their renewed vigor would certainly benefit her yoga practice, when her elbow healed enough for her to go back to the studio. Until then, some nice walks through the neighborhood would do just fine.

"My boss called this morning," said Roland. "He says I'm in the running for a promotion. Something about a special commendation from the CIA." He let his head loll to the left to look at Delphine. "But you're not CIA."

"No, but it's the closest I could get to giving you good feedback without naming our organization."

"Because if she did that, she'd have to kill you," added Kenji.

"You guys need to stop saying things like that," said Roland.

Kenji looked at him with a flat expression. "But it's the truth."

"Stop scaring our new friend, Kenji," said Delphine.

"I was wondering though…" said Roland, hesitating to finish his thought.

"What is it?" Delphine asked.

"Can I come work for you, or maybe be your new partner?" he asked, talking so fast that his words almost ran together.

She laughed. "That certainly is a complete turnaround from your attitude when I picked you up at the airport."

Roland fidgeted in his chair and pulled his feet out of the little soaking tub, resting them on the cement to dry in the sunshine. He looked disappointed, like he'd been trying to plot a move to LA.

"What would your wife think of LA?" asked Kenji. Roland didn't answer.

Delphine shook her head. "It's impossible anyway. I told them no. That's not me anymore. Cased closed."

"You can take the woman out of the spy operation, but you can't take the spy instincts out of the woman," countered Kenji.

"True," she said. "But I'm done with bureaucracy."

"And Sylvie asked you if you wanted to run the Big Cheese operation with her, yes?" asked Kenji.

Roland sat up. "Really?"

"Yes. But as I said, I've no interest in running anything other than my own affairs." Her stomach grumbled. "I would have loved to taste that Beaufort, though."

Kenji smiled and got up from his chair. He walked to the patio table under the pergola, leaving wet footprints behind. When he returned, he was carrying a tray, on which rested a small charcuterie board. He placed it on the patio table in front of them.

Delphine smiled at her old friend. "You sly fox."

# NEXT IN THE SERIES

**Gone Grandpa**

**A fun and witty caper featuring diamonds, deceit … and double-crossing.**

Join Delphine Lougheed and her pals on an Old School romp across SoCal, on the search for someone who might not be who they think he is…

**Pick up your copy at your favorite retailer today!**

# BOOKS BY ANDREA C. NEIL

**OLD SCHOOL MYSTERIES**

The Blingsters

The Big Cheese

Gone Grandpa

The Last Resort

**THE BEVERLEY GREEN ADVENTURES**

Beverley Green's First Adventure

Beverley Green's First Territorial Christmas

Beverley Green Finds True North

Beverley Green Comes Home

The Guthrie Short Stories

**MICRO FICTION**

Days Are Beautiful: 100 flash fiction stories

No Surprises: 100 flash fiction stories

**Visit acneil.com for more information**

# ACKNOWLEDGMENTS

A big cheesy thanks to everyone who helped make this book possible!

Thanks to my business partner, editor, and dear friend Michele Chiappetta, for your patience and insights. You've helped me become a better writer and a better person. Unfortunately, I'm not sure anything can be done about my comma problem.

Ren Bates, thank you for your amazing artwork. You bring my ideas into clearer, more colorful focus. Your generosity and artistic talents are a big part of these stories.

Hooray for Deepti Zaremba for being a fearless beta reader! All those krimis you've read have paid off in the form of excellent story advice.

Many thanks to the early readers for giving me good feedback and waiting (sometimes not very patiently) for me to finish a project! Extra special thanks to Alan Bates and Keith Burns. You guys rock.

Thanks also to Julie Umansky, Kim Yutani, Dayl Workman, Lisa and Bill Neil, Ellie Coppola, Elena Phipps and Lynn Hershman Leeson and the rest of the yoga ladies, and Lisa Bracken. Y'all mean a lot to me, and thanks for all the support.

And last but not least, thank YOU so much for reading this book!

# ABOUT THE AUTHOR

Andrea lives in Oklahoma but grew up in Southern California—and the latter will always be home in her heart. In 2015 she left a job in finance to follow her passion for writing and creating art. With age comes wisdom, or at least a few more stories to tell, and in 2018, Andrea began self-publishing quirky novels with the intention of brightening her readers' day. When she's not trying to get her own words onto a page, Andrea edits other people's writing, eats dark chocolate, and goes on walks if the weather's nice.

acneil.com

amazon.com/author/andreaneil

bookbub.com/profile/andrea-c-neil

facebook.com/andreacneil

instagram.com/andreacneil

www.ingramcontent.com/pod-product-compliance
Lightning Source LLC
Chambersburg PA
CBHW020037310726
48970CB00007B/2288